Traill Hall Publishing

PREY

PREY

J D Currums

Traill Hall Publishing

Paperback ISBN: 978-1-917222-07-5
Ebook ISBN: 978-1-917222-08-2

This work is fictional and any resemblance to actual persons, living or dead is purely coincidental.

Also available from the Author

Condemned - a short story

Death in the Highlands – Crime short story series

In memory of
Wendy Gardner

Prologue – Neil – 01/04/1979

Neil hugged his legs close to him as he sat at the top of the stairs, his tiny feet curled over the edge of the cold wooden step. His toes were chilly, but he was used to it. He had moved carefully past the creaky floorboard to perch, alert and listening to what the police officer, who was talking in hushed tones to his aunt, had to say.

'I'm sorry Maggie, they've vanished I'm afraid. All our enquiries have come up empty. The case will remain open for now, but I can't see any other way forward at present, there just aren't any more leads.'

'Thank you, detective, it's the same thing you told us last time, I wasn't expecting much else. Not sure what I'll tell the boy though. Not sure what I'll do with him either to be honest.'

The missing couple were Maggie's brother Dennis and his wife, Kathleen. Maggie had never been close to her brother but as the only family, had felt pressured to take in their child after they disappeared.

Neil had listened carefully to the conversation. He felt the sting in his eyes as tears streamed his grief down his red and blotchy face. He had hoped they would come back for him.

When the heavy footfall of the detective headed out of the front door, Neil retreated deeper into the shadows of the landing then jumped when the powerful voice of his aunt Maggie boomed up the stairs 'Get to bed. Now!'

Her tone was full of irritation and lacked the tenderness Neil had hoped for when he first met his aunt. The boy shuffled back to his room, his mismatched pyjamas tickling the back of his calves. He'd grown recently but hadn't dared ask for a new pair.

He didn't go to bed. He looked around the cluttered room. He had two options, bed or drawing. He plonked himself down at the desk that was in his room and started drawing in something of a frenzy. Sheet after sheet of paper. He drew similar pictures on each of them; a large house, a man, a woman and a huge sunshine pouring light across the scene. The man in each image was roughly the same, tall, slim and as handsome as Neil could make him.

The woman though, changed in each picture, she had a different look in each one. It was reminiscent of someone playing with fashion plates, designing different 'looks' by swapping sections in and out. First, she had long dark hair and a long dress, next, a short bob and trousers.

Once he'd finished drawing, Neil squashed some Blu Tac between his fingers. It was already soft, so it didn't take much work, and he began to place his pictures on the wall.

Content, he climbed into bed and curled up under his duvet, blocking out the light from his lamp and creating his own tiny sanctuary. He slowly tapped out a rhythm with his fingers. He tapped his thumbs together five times, fore fingers together four times, middle fingers three times, ring fingers twice and finally his two little fingers tapped together, and his eyes closed. It had become something of ritual. He simply couldn't sleep without his countdown. The conclusion of his compulsion was almost mesmeric. He relaxed down into his bed and fell fast asleep.

In the darkest part of the night, Neil woke. Still and terrified and surrounded by a stifling dampness. His cheeks burned as he guessed the cause. He knew Aunt Maggie would be angry, and he was momentarily frozen, not knowing what to do. After a few deep breaths, he crept out onto the landing and slowly opened the airing cupboard where the spare sheets were stored. The warmth enveloped him, more of an embrace than his aunt would contemplate, and he sunk for a moment into the soft heat. When he felt suitably soothed, Neil reached up and brought a cosy striped flannel sheet down and back into his bedroom. He changed the sheet and flipped his duvet over, after all, it hadn't received the brunt of the accident. He then quickly changed into a new pair of pants and a vest; he didn't have another pair of pyjamas. He dropped the soiled pair into the washing basket in the corner and shoved the sheet far under his bed. Out of sight, out of mind. He curled back into bed, still worried that he'd be discovered but hoping he'd hidden his shame as well as he could. He began his finger tapping once again and was soon fast asleep.

When the morning arrived and Neil heard his aunt rising, he sprinted from his bed, dressing at top speed to hide the humiliation of the night before. Maggie didn't look in as she stomped across the hallway and down the stairs, just as she hadn't looked in the night before.

Neil crept down the stairs quietly and hovered in the hall before tiptoeing into the kitchen. Maggie was sat at the kitchen table drinking coffee and leafing through her diary. Neil hovered, unsure whether to go looking for breakfast or whether his aunt would prepare him some. When his parents had first disappeared, Neil had been placed with a foster family. Once his aunt was located, he was transferred but he'd only been there a few days. Neil didn't find his aunt very approachable, but he hoped that would change. It must have been a surprise for her to have him turn up without his parents.

'I wish you wouldn't hover Neil. Sit down.'

Neil scuttered over to the dining table and sat down, allowing his legs to swing back and forth beneath the table and release his nervous energy in the way his aunt would find least irritating. Aunt Maggie soon plonked down a bowl of thick porridge in front of him, with a scattering of brown sugar across the top. She sat opposite Neil, and he could feel her watching him. He felt like one of the penguins in the zoo, stuck in a cage with people watching and directing him. Aunt Maggie looked at him, but she showed no feelings, just a touch of curiosity in the curve of her eyebrow at the creature that was now hers to raise.

'We'll pop to the school later, see if you can start attending. Can't have you hanging around the house all day.'

Neil nodded and smiled, hoping for some sympathy. He used to go to the small Manor Field Primary school where he used to live. He didn't go every day though and hadn't been for a few weeks now. His tummy began to ache as he thought of starting a new school.

As he stared at his aunt, he wondered what had happened to stop her and his dad from staying in touch. He was six and had never met his aunt before now. He hadn't met his mum either. His real mum anyway. He usually lived with his dad and whoever his girlfriend was at the time. Even on his first meeting with a new girlfriend, Neil's dad always insisted that Neil call her 'Mum'. Neil's dad had mostly been kind to him, but he had an unforgiving temper at times. At age six, Neil had witnessed more violence within his home than most people would witness in a lifetime. It happened in terrifying waves. A new girlfriend, a happy few weeks with trips to Clacton and family days by the sea, then slowly the rumbling of arguments would wake Neil in the night, until finally an explosion of rage would see the woman kicked through the front door dripping blood and tears in her wake. Sometimes a police officer would knock, and sometimes not.

On the day when they left, Neil's dad hadn't kicked her out of the door, but there had been blood and tears. Then there had been silence. Neils dad roared at him to go to his room until he said he could leave. Neil always did as he was told, especially when his dad used that voice that echoed through the house. If his dad said he should wait in his room, that was what he did. For four days he had dithered and panicked, but ultimately, he had not dared leave his room. He sat staring forlornly from his window, his dirty clothes soiled and his face sad and neglected. Neil didn't remember it all. He did remember wetting himself when he was in his room but after it went quiet, Neil couldn't quite recall. He remembered feeling hungry.

Neil heard the police say that a neighbour had called them. She'd watched him, hour after hour, day after day. She described him as a 'pale spectre', whatever that meant. The police had told Neil about this neighbour, after they'd kicked the door in and found him. Each time they tried to coax him from the room he screamed and lashed out, terrified of the consequences. Eventually, a police officer came from downstairs and passed Neil a note, he said his dad had asked him to hand it to him. Neil read carefully, he could read a little, but not with the fluency of an older child. *Neil, you can leave your room now. Go with the police and behave*. Once his eyes had finished tracing the words, Neil stepped forward, allowing an officer to wrap him in a blanket and lead him down the stairs. It was only later that Neil wondered whether the note was actually from his father. The policeman wore blue plastic gloves and Neil wondered if it was because he thought he was dirty and didn't want to catch anything.

The sterile police station was dull, but the policeman bought Neil a burger and milkshake which brightened him up a little. While he ate, the policeman asked about his parents. Neil said he hadn't seen them in days but nothing else. He knew better than to speak to anyone about his dad. Instead, he sat and watched and listened to snatched conversations in the hallway. He built up his own understanding of what happened, without having to say a word. The police kept referring to the woman that had been in the house, his dad's girlfriend, as Neil's mother. Clearly they didn't know that Neil's mother had run away and left him behind when he was a baby.

PART ONE

1 - Jasper – 05/06/1996

Like a worm in his gut, gnawing savagely from the inside out, Jasper felt the torment of failure. She'd left only minutes ago, Jasper had been too slow to stop her and now he needed to make some quick decisions. Jasper ran around gathering his things and cleaning where he needed to. Now his bag was ready, he couldn't afford to wait any longer.

He twitched the curtains and peeked out from the shadows. Satisfied nobody was waiting for him, he silently opened the door of the large and magnificent property and slid out, shutting the door silently behind him. He edged round the cars parked on the road, using them to camouflage his departure. He avoided the main roads and kept to the back streets. Once away from the vicinity of the house, he moved his pace up into a run, strong and rhythmic.

Sweat dripped from Jasper's forehead and pooled in darkening patches on his t-shirt, particularly around the straps of his backpack, as he ran towards Weymouth train station. Nobody was pursuing him. Yet. When he saw the door of the ticket office he bent double. Panting, Jasper stopped long enough to regain his equilibrium. He ducked behind the bins and allowed himself to settle. He crouched low and pulled his bag from his back, withdrawing a fresh t-shirt and quickly swapped out the moist one, with its sweat patches. He spritzed a little body spray across his clothing and took a few deep breaths, hoping now he would blend in.

Jasper walked into the train station, a well prepared, confident smile on his lips, and approached the ticket desk, while giving a cursory glance at the departure board. The next train was due in four minutes and terminated at Castle Cary. Jasper had no idea where this was, but it would do for now.

'Where are you heading?' asked the man behind the desk, a grumpy disposition hiding behind his faux smile.

'Castle Cary please, single.' Jasper replied, tilting his head down slightly to allow some of his long hair to fall across his face.

The man nodded and soon dispatched a ticket. 'Platform two, six minutes'.

Jasper handed over cash for the ticket and grabbed his change along with the ticket. He strode hurriedly over to platform two. Once there, he shuffled backwards, behind a hefty potted plant. It wasn't tall, so he squatted down and rested, out of line of sight from most of the other passengers. He'd only rested a couple of minutes before the train rolled into the station.

Jasper reached his destination and took a further two trains, heading gradually west, still not entirely sure of his destination. Just before his final change, he had seen a tourist map, tatty and probably filthy, laying on a seat across from him. He tentatively picked it up by the edges, spreading it out. There were small square tags showing tourist hotspots. They seemed to be overflowing in one small seaside town. *St Afan* Jasper thought. *Why not?*

Jasper stepped off the stuffy train several hours after his journey began. Sea salt-drenched air mixed with the delicious aromas floating from the nearby restaurants, taunting him; it had been hours since he'd nibbled some toast in the morning, and he was ravenous. He paused and inhaled, determination showing in the set of his mouth, food would come later, once he decided if he was staying.

He strode down the platform and on into town, appraising the potential. Lots of bars and nightclubs, and a lively young crowd from the looks of those sauntering through the streets. He could still move on elsewhere of course, but so far, the town looked perfect. His shoulders began to relax for the first time since he'd left the house that morning. The relief of having left undetected released tension from his muscles. He was frustrated and angry this morning but now, he wondered whether he had to fail to come to this little haven by the sea where he was sure he could try again. This morning his cool had slipped, and panic had taken over but now, at this end of the day, he felt he was back in control.

The town was larger than he'd expected with a lively atmosphere. Street vendors sold tourist oddments and candy floss. There were posters for water sports and desks where you could sign up. As he continued to walk, he saw what he needed - a barber shop. It was luckily quiet with one person in the chair and nobody waiting. He gently pulled at the band holding his long hair back and allowed it to fall down next to his face.

When the previous customer stood and vacated the chair, the barber gave a quick and not very effective brush of the chair and floor. Jasper breathed deep, ignoring how many previous customers' hairs would soon be clinging to him. He sat in the chair, stiff and uncomfortable, knowing it needed to be done. When the barber stood behind him, full of bouncy energy and extra-large smiles, Jasper tried to match his energy and expression as he asked for a cut. 'Short back and sides, undercut but longer on top, so it reaches down to here.' Jasper indicated the bottom of his cheek bones.

'Got it, we'll get you neatened up in minutes.'

That jaunty energy grated on Jasper, but he played along, eyes twinkling and head nodding at the inane attempts at conversation. When Jasper walked out of the barber shop, he was amazed how different he looked with his hair chopped.

Next, he dipped into a clothing shop, containing a variety of shirts and semi-formal wear. Jasper selected some shirts and tank tops. He paid cash and left, heading to the public toilets. When he emerged, he looked worlds apart from the man that arrived in St Afan a short while before. His change in appearance allowed him to relax and he could now begin looking for opportunities.

He walked on and saw several people wearing yellow vests and looks of hope as they approached passers-by. Walking close to one, he saw that they were collecting for a local animal shelter and signing people up for regular donations. He turned and rotated three hundred and sixty degrees, surveying what he was now beginning to consider his territory, before turning back to the yellow vested lady. She was probably in her forties, wiry build and a grim expression when she wasn't turning it on for a customer. Jasper doubted she did well with sign-ups, unless people paid her to leave them alone.

'Do they pay well to have you out here all day?' Jasper flashed his most loveable smile.

'Minimum wage, but it's easy work out in the sun.'

Jasper smiled at the woman who stared miserably back at him and slowly retreated. He knew what he needed to do next.

This time he would succeed.

06/06/1996

For his first night in St Afan, Jasper had found a backpacker's hostel. It was communal and grim and smelt of dirty bodies and sweaty feet. He clenched his teeth at the thought of having to stay another night there. He needed to find an alternative, quickly. He had briefly noticed a couple of community notice boards on his arrival but hadn't looked properly in his hurry to alter his appearance. He headed first to the beachside where the notes on the board waved gently in the warm breeze, the tatters on some attesting to the wilder weather earlier in the season. There were a couple of jobs posted and a house share. It wasn't quite what he was looking for, so he moved on towards the grand old building at the end of the High Street which was used as the town hall.

This time, his eyes lit up at a fresh sheet of white paper pinned on the board. It looked pristine and like it had only just been added. *Urgent - House sitter needed in Afan View Farm – care of some small animals and general basic upkeep (gardening etc.).* There were several copies of the phone number at the bottom of the sheet, intended to be torn off individually. Jasper took the entire sheet from the board, there was no sense in encouraging competition.

***

Jasper walked from the town centre gently uphill on the winding roads leading to Afan View Farm. The neat town roads edged with curb stones slowly turned into single track country roads with no pavements and no lighting. He wouldn't need the lights until later of course, but it was useful to know the lay of the land. The sun blazed down and as he approached the farm, he could detect the slight sting of sunburn on his forehead. He made a mental note to find sunscreen later. A wooden sign marked the entrance and Jasper paused to assess the premises from afar, before he approached and would surely be observed.

The farmhouse was surrounded by fields. It was hard to believe that they'd be worked by the current owners, they'd sounded elderly when Jasper had telephoned. It would be something he would have to find out. The farmhouse itself stood in a plot of around an acre, which was mostly overgrown gardens, filled with colour and was a messy wilderness. It also housed a large barn behind the house, only partially visible from his location. Jasper walked down the rough driveway and could see the signs that the upkeep of the farmhouse was taking its toll on the owners. Little jobs had begun to be left undone. Guttering still overloaded with last year's leaves. Peeling paintwork on the windows and porch. The garden taken over by weeds, the fence post long since broken.

Stepping up to the wooden porch door, Jasper knocked in the perkiest rhythm he could manage and hitched his winning smile onto his face, eyes a little wider than usual. A picture of innocence.

An elderly woman answered the door, grey hair in a twist at the back of her head and a summery dress floating to her ankles. Her face was sun-darkened and wrinkled, but her eyes twinkled with kindness. A man's grey stubbled face appeared over his wife's shoulder, a wide smile on his lips.

'Hi, my name is Jasper, I called about the house-sitting job for the summer. I'm working for the local animal shelter, fundraising. It doesn't pay well so I'd be really keen to take the role if it's still available.'

He'd barely finished speaking when he realised they'd already been hooked by his faux charm, and were nodding along. 'Come on in son, let's have a pot of tea and we can figure out how it will work.'

Jasper nodded warmly and followed them into their home. He had nowhere else to stay and couldn't afford for them to change their minds, so his charm offensive continued for the next hour while they probed him about the details of the fictitious CV he'd handed them. 'Where are you from? Seems a lot of different places on your references.'

'We moved around a lot, just my Mum and me but she died last year.' Jasper performed this well, looking down, dabbing at the corner of his eye and standing for a walk about the room. He didn't want to overplay it, but he wanted an end to the questions.

After the interrogation was complete, the old gentleman took Jasper on a tour of the property. The house held three bedrooms and was dated but standard in layout. Next, he showed him out of the back door to a large barn, unlocking it with an oversized plank of wood that was held on brackets horizontally to bar the door. Once removed, double doors swung open revealing a large space, neatly organised but filled with many relics of when the farm was in full use. 'You shouldn't need much in here but the mowers over there, and most of the basic tools, hammers, screwdrivers and things are all on these shelves.'

Jasper suspected that the old man was worried an urgent repair might be necessary and wanted to ensure Jasper knew where to find what he needed. 'Just beware of that' he said, signalling a large piece of plywood on the floor that seemed to be sagging in the centre. 'It's a pit for looking at cars but we don't use it. I think the wood's a bit old now, so I wouldn't stand on it.'

Jasper smiled and nodded, while also surveying what else was hidden in the barn. The tools were standard. A stack of cable ties sat limply in a tray and all sorts of ropes and harnesses too. 'What do you use these for?'

The old man looked at the ropes Jasper had alluded to. 'We used to run a campsite, and the young folks came for the climbing on the local cliffs. Some of them left equipment after they departed. We kept it in case it was needed by anyone else. In truth, they've sat there for about fifteen years now. I should probably get rid of them, but they're not in the way, so I've just left them. If you want to use them, you can.'

The old man ambled back out of the door and waited while Jasper exited, before heaving the bar back onto the brackets, sealing the door.

The pair strolled across the expansive lawn and back into the farmhouse. 'The chickens there need to be back in their houses in the evening, or the fox will get them. The goat can stay out, he's got a shelter. I'll write down what to feed them and when.' Jasper nodded along as Mr

Glamcoe gave his instructions.

At the end of the meeting, it had been agreed that Jasper would come and see them off the following morning. They would leave contact numbers for him and some money. Additional payment would be made on their return. They also agreed to put Jasper on the insurance for their second car. They wouldn't need it, and it would make life easier for Jasper. 'Mr and Mrs Glamcoe, thank you so much for giving me this chance, I will take good care of the place. If there's any odd jobs that need doing over the summer, you leave a list, and I'll do what I can with those too.'

With that, Jasper left, strolling down the long driveway, crunching on the gravel beneath his feet and enjoying the view from high up on the cliffs. He was also smiling at the perfection of this location, a beautiful, quiet place where he wouldn't be disturbed.

2 – Ria – 10/06/1996

Ria plucked chocolate pop tarts from the toaster while her nose remained buried in an essay she had written and re-written repeatedly over the last few weeks. She had twenty minutes before she needed to leave for her holiday, and the essay was due two days after her return. She hunched over the kitchen table surrounded by papers, her head shaking minutely side to side in dissatisfaction at what she was reading. It still wasn't right. After ferociously rifling through the pages, she still had no clear idea of how to move forward. She slammed the palms of her hands down on the table, overwhelmed by her inability to meet her own inflated expectations.

Ria pulled her bag towards her, withdrew two small white pills from a pack and swallowed them with water, before finally munching on her breakfast. Her mother would be home soon, and Ria was aiming to be packed up and gone before she got back. Her father would be out for most of the day, which was a shame as she would have loved more time with him. Him, not her. Every car she heard on the road outside caused her to pause and listen, hoping it was not her mum. She'd prefer to dart to her room rather than hear the standard overtures of disappointment from her.

The holiday was to St Afan in Cornwall with its promise of sun, sea and apparently endless booze to keep her and her friends occupied. The coach would take about five hours, and Ria decided she would have to work on the journey there. The fear of failure was weighing her down. After the journey, she promised herself, she would put her work away and try to just have fun. Shuffling papers together and trying to draw a line under her agitation, she raced upstairs and dressed in record time. She spritzed some body spray across herself and her clothes, filling the room with a cloying sweetness. Then she grabbed a large green camping backpack and stuffed it full of clothes and filled a small bag with her study notes. She then dived under her bed, to the furthest barely reachable corner and withdrew a stack of letters, stuffing them deep into her rucksack. She was downstairs again within ten minutes. Satisfied, she pulled her black Doc Martens on and laced them up. She'd packed flip-flops and sandals in her bag for the warmer weather she hoped to find at their destination.

The radio in the kitchen was still blaring with sounds of Gina G and 'Just a little bit'. Ria screwed up her face and switched channel, she didn't mind pop music but preferred a bit more substance, ideally a guitar or two. The sounds of Baddiel, Skinner and the Lightning Seeds blasted to life from the speaker. 'Three Lions' was certain to be playing in all the pubs and clubs in the lead up to the Euro's. Ria found herself humming along, other than the chorus, the words hadn't quite sunk in yet since its release.

After a brief musical interlude, she sat a while longer, head in hands, trying to calm her heart and breathing. The stress was getting out of control. She was looking forward to a holiday and certainly to some secret plans she'd put in place, but she was dreading the antics her friends would try to pull her into. They were primary school friends that seemed to stick. Ria pondered how it was often the people who know you the best that could apply the most pressure. They didn't understand that her moral compass was a little more complicated than theirs seemed to be. Callie particularly had been getting wilder by the day. Standing and shrugging, Ria hitched on her pack and was ready. She would just have to learn to stand up to them, she decided. She stepped out of the door, letting it close and lock behind her. She stood at the end of the paved driveway, just as Callie and Olivia bobbed into sight.

Ria watched as Callie's sleek black hair bounced in time with her movements. She always managed to pull off *effortless cool* and Ria could never quite grasp how. There was always a somewhat sullen edge to her expression, even when she laughed. A *don't mess with me* message that showed consistently in all she did. The opposite of Olivia really. Olivia was pretty, but she didn't ever really believe it. She was tiny and almost always wore her hair in two long plaits. When she let it out at night, she always reminded Ria of a mermaid who'd come ashore. Particularly fitting when the dark smear of eye liner became blurry and smudged. There was a hesitance in Olivia's movements, her piercing green blue eyes flicked all about her like a nervous bird emerging from the nest and expecting to be attacked. *What do they think when they look at me?* Ria pondered before deciding she did not care and that she prioritised cultivating her mind.

The three girls greeted each other and wove down the road, nudging each other and laughing. Ria watched the excitement emanating from her friends and felt exhilarated and ready to let loose, at least a little. She knew this holiday would be their last together before they went their separate ways when Ria went to university and her two friends began work.

'Seriously, this is going to break my back' Callie said dramatically causing Ria to laugh.

'You want to swap bags for a bit?' Olivia chipped in. Ria knew Olivia would do anything for Callie.

Callie jumped in front of her, looking down at her from her elevation of five inches taller, 'Liv, you're tiny, this would break you.'

'I'm small, I'm not weak. You crack on though.' Olivia returned, looking a little peeved compared to moments before. Ria smiled, happy that it was Olivia's turn to be teased for a change, she knew how much Olivia hated being judged as small and weak due to her height. She loved Olivia and didn't want her upset, but she was glad of a break in the teasing of which she normally took the brunt.

They walked out of town, away from the neat estate where the three of them lived. They moved onto a broad road lined with mature oak trees, rustling gently in the cool breeze of freedom. They were collecting Molly on their way to the coach and if they carried on past her house, they would soon end up in the lush Oxfordshire countryside.

'I don't know how I'm going to cope with a week away from revision, especially as I haven't finished the final essay yet.' Ria was staring intently ahead, visualising the mountain of work still awaiting her.

'You already know it all, what's left to revise? Besides, I haven't even started my essay yet.' Callie sneered slightly at her friend. Ria knew that Callie always got angry with her when she was over-zealous about study.

'You can't be too prepared' snapped back Ria. 'What would I actually do if I failed? I can do it; it would be a shame to let myself down by being lazy wouldn't it?'

'If you say so' Callie had apparently become instantly bored of the exchange and upped her pace. 'Come on, we need to dash and grab Molly or we're gonna miss the coach.'

With that, the girls tightened their hold on their overstuffed bags and jogged the last few metres, landing on the steps in front of Molly's large, double-fronted home and dropping their luggage. Callie approached the heavy wooden door, hammering on it and leaving Molly no choice but to hear and hurry up. While they waited for her, Ria paced the driveway, muttering a poem from her English set texts under her breath as she watched Callie sprawl on the steps and Olivia standing still, looking somewhat awkward.

Molly threw open her front door and exhaled a sigh that Ria read as relief. 'I'll just grab my bags' she called out of the open door. Ria could hear the pounding of her feet as she ran back up the stairs, collecting her luggage and ran down again, slamming the door behind her. On the steps outside, Molly dumped her bags and sat down, retrieving her tobacco tin from her pocket and extracting a pre-rolled joint. Sparking up, she handed the spliff to Callie who accepted 'Get your bags, we need to move,' Callie ordered from the side of her mouth while the cigarette hung limply. Callie inhaled deeply as she ushered her friends forward. Ria looked on but said nothing, trying to remove the frown she could feel creasing forehead.

They loaded up, and marched down the hill, in companionable silence, passing the joint between them. Ria barely inhaled anything before passing it on but decided to continue with the charade rather than be mocked for being a square again. As they approached the coach stop, Ria was looking at her friends, chatting when she saw their faces drop in unison. Turning, Ria saw the coach doors beginning to close. Callie, the most athletic, sprinted ahead, covering the space in seconds, and pounded on the door. The driver gave a friendly smile and re-opened them. He then jumped down, allowing their larger bags to be stowed beneath. As the girls lingered outside for their bags to be loaded into the luggage compartment, the driver puffed from the exertion of leaning into it. Ria smiled to herself as Olivia inched closer to the coach driver. 'Do you want a hand?' Olivia offered.

'No thanks, Miss. Jump aboard and I'll be in for tickets in a minute.' His words were reassuring but the reddening of his face from exertion was not. Ria saw Olivia's crestfallen face and knew she felt most comfortable when she was helping someone else.

Ria watched as Olivia turned away and was the first to hop on the coach. Ria stepped on quickly behind her. Olivia wore blue corduroy trousers and a two-tone vest top. She certainly looked trendier than Ria did in her neat and tidy tailored shorts and loose white shirt. Olivia never went anywhere without her portable compact disc player. She had her Discman clipped to the back of her trousers, ready to block out the world for the long journey ahead. She also carried a bag containing cans of cider for the friends to share. Olivia shoved it under her seat. Ria sat on a double seat opposite, she knew that her place was not with Olivia. Ria watched as Callie strolled onto the bus and slid in next to Olivia, the casualness of her movements reflecting her character. Ria knew she was happy to make people wait for her. She had sunglasses perched on her head and Ria could see the greenish hue of her face. She knew that vomit would follow before long. Callie often remarked that she was 'growing out' of her travel sickness but sadly for her friends, it didn't look to be declining yet, and despite the name, it often began before she left home.

The coach driver checked the girls' tickets, eyeing them from under a uniform flat cap. Molly had taken longer than the others to embark. She stood to the side of the door, finishing her spliff. Ria kept peering down the aisle, frowning and hoping she would drop it and get on board. Ria watched as Molly eventually jumped up the steps. Eyes hidden behind dark glasses, long hair free and wild. She bounced along, a happy air emanating with every step. As with Olivia's cords, Molly's flared jeans had a worn patch at the back where they were just slightly too long and spent most of their time getting stomped on by her flip-flops. Ria shrunk towards the window, allowing Molly space to settle next to her. She watched as Molly took an old and well-worn book from her bag and began to read. Ria glanced sideways, noting symbols she associated with paganism and devil worship. She flared her nostrils and took a deep breath, trying her best not to react. She was distracted on the journey by the constant presence on her friend's lap, of this book, and the thoughts of what was to come.

The road drove a path through the patchwork of green fields that had surrounded their childhood. They were striking out and ready for their first adult holiday. Ria watched as the shades of green outside the window blurred before her eyes, mesmerising her. She tried and failed to block out the repetitive guitar riffs she could hear buzzing from Olivia's headphones. Every now and then, Ria watched as Molly tapped Olivia's shoulder to show her a section of the book she seemed to be obsessed with. She knew Callie would be as irritated by this as she was.

By the time they were passing Bodmin, Callie had vomited three times. Thankfully into a pre-prepared bag. Olivia took the deposits to the coach toilets, but she swapped places with Callie early in the trip so she could at least turn away from the vomit splatter when it was happening. The regular heaving and stench had certainly ended any thoughts of cracking out the cans of cider they'd brought. In her moments after vomiting, Callie seemed to get a new lease of life. She would casually throw a 'would you rather' question to the group. 'So, Jamie Redknapp or Paul Ince?'

'Clearly Ince' Olivia threw back before replacing her headphones.

'Schmeichel or Seaman?'

'Shoot me now! No more Cal, please!' Ria laughed as Olivia shuffled sideways, facing the aisle, and turned the volume on her Discman up even further. She knew they were best friends, but sometimes they obviously needed to be tuned out.

3 – Olivia – 10/06/1996

The coach pulled into the bus station of St Afan. Olivia looked longingly at a taxi rank nearby that attracted many of their fellow passengers, but they were on a student budget. Donning their enormous backpacks they headed off. Olivia watched Ria leading the way until she suddenly stopped. Olivia could tell she had no idea where she was going and then she confirmed it.

'Molly, do you know where to go' Ria asked her friend. Her face showed that she hated being on the back foot.

Olivia could never fathom her need to know everything all the time. She really needed to learn to go with the flow. Sometimes it was alright to let others take the lead, particularly when the others were your friends and not the creepy guys your Mum has brought home.

Molly nodded and skipped off, taking a quick left heading across the High Street and into a road heading uphill, parallel to the coast. Molly's independent nature nurtured an innate sense of direction which Olivia and the others were generally happy to follow.

Olivia had noticed a change in Ria lately. She was always reluctant to share anything personal but now Olivia felt she was hiding something more than she normally did. She'd only just got a mobile phone a few months ago and rarely used it, especially if she was with her friends. Who else would she call? Ria trudged along behind her and Olivia cast surreptitious glances backwards as often as she could, undetected. Olivia saw Ria withdraw her phone and shoot off a message, a smile creeping into her expression. Olivia thought Ria's movements had become jittery and excited, but the excitement held a separate space to that of her friends.

Olivia said nothing and kept walking, but she began to wonder, what was it that was changing with Ria and who would she be texting? Olivia knew Ria's parents didn't have mobile phones. As Olivia considered what Ria's secret could be, her eyes lifted, and she saw a man watching from a bench in the centre of the High Street. When she looked, he averted his eyes, but he had been watching, that much she was sure of. Well, maybe they'd meet him later, he was young and good looking, and she hoped to see more of him.

They traipsed up the hill from the town centre, up into the residential streets overlooking the ocean. Olivia loved that each house was painted in beautiful shades of pastel. When they were high up, Olivia breathed deep, enjoying the views across the bustling seaside town and coastline beyond. Molly finally stopped at the front door of an old cottage with an attractive, well-tended garden, bursting with flowers of every colour. Even with the tang of sea salt in the air, the flower scent was strong and sweet. Olivia watched Callie's recovery with every breath she took. The fresh, clear air had revived her from several hours of sickness and returned her skin tone to a more natural hue. Olivia was glad she didn't get travel sick but wished she'd recover as quickly as Callie when she was ill.

A lady answered the door, Olivia considered her old, probably her mum's age. She thought she was beautiful though with a freckled face and a warm smile. Olivia turned away with Callie and Ria, allowing Molly to sort out the practicalities. They stood in the beautiful garden, satisfied that they had escaped parents and rules and this was the beginning of an amazing week. Olivia shot glances at Callie often. She always wanted to gain her approval and have Callie on her side. After Molly handed the lady the final balance for their stay, she was given a single set of keys which Molly slipped into her pocket. Olivia stepped closer to Molly now and they were directed back down the hill to the holiday cottage that would be their home for the week.

Olivia knew how good Molly was at playing the

innocent young woman to adults, so she was happy to leave her to do the talking. Now, trudging back downhill, Olivia felt freer. She felt the laughter jump from her lips at the slightest encouragement. They'd done it, they'd arrived, and Olivia intended to enjoy every second.

When they arrived, sweaty and exhausted, Olivia stood back while Molly opened up. Stepping inside Olivia crinkled her nose, the musty salt smell seemed to penetrate everywhere within the cottage.

The floorboards squawked to life with each new step, down the pink runner. Threads trailing on the wood to either side, Olivia made a mental note to avoid the trip hazards. She was always clumsy despite trying so hard not to be. Olivia watched her friends elbowing each other to be at the front as they raced up the stairs and practically fell into the bedroom. Olivia followed behind, reading the wooden plaque on the bedroom door, *Chenowet*. She read it more than once before deciding how to pronounce it. Testing it in her mouth through repetition. She wondered if it had a meaning or whether it was just the owner's name.

A mantelpiece stood, centred on the far wall, closed off with a wooden board. On the floor sat a blue and white china jug, filled to the top with shades of blue, purple and brown pot-pourri. It looked like the kind of thing Olivia's Granny would have in her house. She couldn't smell it over the salty mustiness ingrained in everything. A single bed sat either side of the door and in the far corner, to the left of the fireplace stood a bunk bed.

Each bed was neatly made with stiff white sheets and blankets, tucked in with military precision. On each pillow, folded identically, was a fluffy pink towel, with a large flower embroidered into the corner. The towels were thick and comforting and the embroidery felt wonderfully homely and was clearly sewn by hand. Olivia loved it when there was a personal touch. Something to make her think of cosy old ladies and hours spent sewing by the fire. She never said this kind of thing out loud though, as her friends would probably tease her.

'Dibs!' screeched Molly, jumping haphazardly up onto the top bunk bed. Olivia threw her bag onto the bunk underneath and sat down. Olivia watched as Callie chose one of the single beds and Ria, as usual, had whatever was left.

Olivia inwardly groaned as no sooner had they set their packs down than Callie withdrew a warm cider from her bag and drank it down, more or less in one. She was a sickly traveller but thankfully recovered quickly. Olivia and the others dutifully followed suit, albeit a little slower. Moving back downstairs, Olivia sat in a wing backed chair, feeling regal, while her friends slouched down on a well-worn sofa. Olivia kicked off her shoes and sweaty socks and let the travel weariness drain from her.

'Right, before we head out then, how about we dish out some fun for the week? We could each have a dare, and punishments if you don't do it!' When Callie finished speaking, Olivia clinked cans with her, cheeky grins spreading through the group.

'Maybe we each write two possibilities and put them in a cup and then we pick and have to do it? That way, you are at risk of doing whatever you put in so it can't be too ridiculous!' Olivia could see the colour rise in Ria's cheeks as she said this, an edge of terror in her eyes.

Olivia tore a page from her sketchbook and handed everyone two small strips, a twinkle in her eye telling all that she knew what she was writing down. Olivia loved silly games. She didn't mind making a fool of herself, providing she felt included.

Before long, Olivia grabbed a chipped blue cup from the kitchen and offered it round to be filled with folded slips of paper. Once they were all in, Olivia swirled the pieces of paper with her fingertips, ensuring they were well mixed.

'Madam' Olivia mock-bowed at Ria, offering her the cup, grin splitting her face in two. She loved this kind of thing.

'Who put skinny-dipping in?' Ria squealed, visibly shrinking into herself at the thought of it.

'That would be me, gimme the pot' Callie leant forward and took hers, smiling. Olivia knew she relished any excuse for pushing boundaries. 'Kiss three guys from different continents. Piece of cake!' she made kisses into the air, clearly enjoying her challenge. 'Liv, what are you gonna be doing?'

Olivia reached in and pulled out a very tightly folded piece of paper. By the time she'd unravelled it, she was squinting to read between the creases. 'Neck five tequilas....now!' Olivia groaned, she was not known for her high tolerance of booze. 'Molls, you pick before I destroy myself'.

Molly leaned in and placed her fingers into the cup. Waiting a moment, she pulled one out 'adopt a traffic cone. Hmmm, ok'. Olivia could see the disappointment on Molly's face, she usually enjoyed a dare or two and this was tame for her.

'Shall we go for a dip before anything else?' Olivia suggested to nods of assent.

They quickly located their swimsuits and edged into discreet corners to dress quickly. 'Unless you want to leave your swimsuit behind Ria!' Olivia bellowed before tripping over and ending up with two legs in one hole of her swimsuit.

Having declined Olivia's kind offer, Ria donned her swimsuit like the rest.

Olivia watched, resigned, as Callie lined up a tequila each for them, plus an additional four for her. She'd even brought salt and lemon to do it properly. They all shouted cheers as they downed their shot, faces moving through a series of emotions before finally scrunching as the sourness from the lemon hit hard. Olivia saw the sparkling eyes of her friends, one shot was enough to get them going. They watched as she downed another four shots in quick succession. By the time they were heading out, Olivia could feel her legs failing her. She felt like Bambi on ice and leant into her friends to help her regain balance.

'The air will sort her out' Callie's voice boomed out. Olivia hoped she was right.

Olivia enjoyed the feeling of the sun on her skin as she walked with her friends, down towards the sea. She was pleased with how healthy and glowing her newly sun screened skin looked and felt a passing warm glow about this. Tramping across the sand, they flicked off their sandals between hops and steps, and Olivia toppled over into the soft sand before getting back to her feet. She dived straight into the clear, cool sea, outer clothes strewn frivolously in a trail of abandonment. Splashing and laughing, they allowed any tension to fall away. Olivia noticed that even Ria, who found it hard to relax, was now smiling contentedly. Their laughter rang freely under the clear blue skies. The beach was busy, and Olivia's eyes glided over the sun-kissed bodies, always looking for something, or someone to captivate her.

The afternoon was spent with drinks and exploring the town. Olivia enjoyed the freedom to just mooch her way through the day, no plan needed. There were many back streets to see, each with quirky shops and postcard views across the bay. They shared a couple of cones of chips at lunchtime, vinegar dripping onto their hands through the bottom which Olivia could smell on her fingers and clothes for the rest of the afternoon.

As the sun dipped lower towards the horizon, their energies dropped too. They needed a break before the evening and headed back to their cottage, ready to prepare. They'd brought packets of super noodles and bean feasts with them which were prepped in no time, it was what Olivia's mum called 'student food' and something she normally only ate when her mum was too busy with the next new man in her life.

Olivia was happy to make the dinner, it took no time, and they were all then feeling more rested and gearing up for the evening. They had quick showers and dressed up for the night, each in their own version of what was the right look. Although nearly women, they still had the rounded faces of youth and Olivia knew they needed some make-up to disguise it.

Olivia sat, desperately trying not to blink while Molly drew on her eye liner before they swapped and she reciprocated. Olivia's hand trembled as she tried to do a neat line with a flick on her friend's eyelids. Eventually, she stepped back, satisfied they were roughly even.

When they finished in the bathroom, Olivia found Callie with a can of cider, headbanging to an Offspring song, dressed in a shiny green skirt and black vest top, glittery green eye shadow smeared on and sparkling as she moved. It only ever took her minutes to get ready. Meanwhile Ria sat, scribbling at the table in the kitchen, sipping gently at a cup of tea, intent on the work spread out in front of her. She was ready to leave wearing a summery dress that was pretty, but more conservative than her friends.

Olivia thought Molly looked beautiful in her sparkly sandals with a long skirt and a strappy top. Olivia had squeezed herself into a tight double layer dress, high at the top and down to the knee, paired with chunky black platform sandals. She appraised herself in the mirror, trying to assess if her belly looked too big or whether some idiot would be able to pull the top of her dress down. Roughly satisfied, the four prepared to leave.

They'd scouted the pubs and clubs earlier in the day

and knew roughly where they were headed. In any case, Olivia was happy to follow the others. The darkness across the bay was interposed with sparkling reflections of the lights from the bars and cafes, the reflections moving in time as the waves crashed. Olivia felt like anything was possible.

Olivia had saved for this holiday but still, money was tight as a student, and she'd rather spend money on fun things than wasting it on eating out or pricey drinks in clubs. They had pre-loaded on Gin Fizz at the cottage. As such, by the time they tottered down to their first pub stop, Olivia was already well on the way to a messy night, staggering onwards in her platform heels.

They entered a lively pub with music spilling out into the street. They sat at a large round table, raised slightly from the level of the rest of the pub. Olivia went to the bar while Molly ordered four bottles of alcopops in different flavours. They were easy to drink, they could have been lemonade. Olivia hoped she wouldn't get obliterated too early. She'd only just recovered from the tequila shots when they'd arrived.

As they were nearing the end of their first round, a group of lads had drifted closer and Olivia watched quietly as Molly and Callie, were soon leaning in close and clearly enjoying the attention. Before long, Molly and Callie were standing up chatting, and two of the guys from the group had shuffled into the circular booth next to Olivia and Ria. Olivia and the closest man, Stephen, began chatting happily, but Olivia noticed that Ria barely spoke to her designated partner and mostly sat looking away and trying her best to keep a gap between them. The man with Ria, Matt, didn't look overly interested either. It was always hard to be the last choice in these situations and somehow Ria always was. Olivia pondered this for a moment, as she considered Ria to be beautiful and independent. She liked how she could stand up to people in a way Olivia never could. Stephen soon regained Olivia's attention, and they were swiftly locked in a steamy embrace, moving as one, hands and tongues exploring freely, despite the public location. Olivia was only brought back to earth when Matt, clearly unhappy with his lot, grabbed his friend's shoulder, interrupting the couple's spontaneous passions, and guided his friend away. The other two men, Nathan and Simon, went with them, ending the first flirtations of the evening for now. 'I bet we'll be seeing them again, they're here all week too.' Olivia said this and noticed how Molly smiled at the thought of it. Olivia would happily see Stephen again and it seemed Molly would certainly like to see more of Simon. She pondered this for a while, thinking of ways to 'bump into them' again.

The evening continued and they moved towards a club, ready to dance the night away. Before they entered, Ria stopped. 'I've got a migraine starting. If I go to bed now it'll be fine but if I don't, it'll ruin tomorrow too. I'll leave the door unlocked for you.' With that, Ria walked away from her friends, heading towards their holiday cottage, and presumably a cool dark room. Olivia and the others watched her leave before turning and continuing with their night.

4 - Jasper - 08/06/1996

Jasper left the vets' office clutching a yellow vest and a clipboard. He knew he interviewed well; he was able to read people and turn on the charm to their exact frequency. He hadn't expected getting the job to be quite so easy. He understood why. Most of the wages were based on commission so it was relatively low risk for the charity. It was high risk for Jasper, in a way, but he knew there was food already at the farmhouse if needed, so he wasn't desperate for the money.

He walked down to the High Street and found a spot, near to the bank, that provided a good vista of each direction. There was a pagoda in the centre of the pedestrianised street, covering a circular formation of benches and consequently that area of the High Street felt more open. The pagoda held planters that were in full bloom, the sweetness of the flowers adding their aromas to the sea salted air.

It was just after noon and the sun was high and strong. Jasper pulled his cap down low over his eyes, he didn't wish to burn any further. He watched as groups of lads and girls emerged, red eyed and slack in their movements, clearly searching for their hangover cure. Couples strolled hand in hand, slow and leisurely and basking in the hot sun. There were short skirts and pale legs and lots of strappy tops. There were signs everywhere that the day was almost unbearably hot. Fanning hands, dabbing tissues and floppy hats wherever he looked.

He shook his head, deterring himself from 'people watching' and decided he needed to get some sign-ups before moving onto his actual agenda. He fitted his smile, scanned the crowd, this time specifically looking for those that might help. His first thought was those with dogs, but it was too hot for dogs to be out on the hot pavement. He drew a blank and began a more random approach, hoping his charm would get him through.

Two hours on and Jasper had obtained six sign-ups – he'd been told not to expect more than one an hour, so he was pleased with his efforts. He sat back on one of the benches and rewarded himself with a cold drink and a more casual survey of the scenes around him. Through a gap in the terraced shop buildings, Jasper could see the coming and going of buses and coaches, dropping off yet more tourists to the town and taking away those that were worn out from pleasure and over-indulgence. The bus station was mostly hidden behind a row of shops but the swarms of people coming and going made it obvious when buses were due.

He noticed a group of four girls, young women really. Something chaotic in the way that they banded together and drifted apart, like the organised chaos of ants. One of the girls was Asian, with long silky black hair that Jasper felt he would love to drape across his fingers. She seemed to lead the others, not necessarily by being at the front, but when she spoke, the others all paid attention. The girl with plaits particularly seemed to hang on her every word. The look in her eye, the adoration appealed to Jasper. One of the others had the vibe of a free spirit, constantly moving and swirling and laughing, her long hair flying with every turn. Jasper loved the freedom in her but a part of him also wanted to block it, to control it. Then there was the other one. *The odd one out* he thought. She seemed calmer, neater, more orderly in every way. As they walked, the orderly one was a little behind and Jasper watched as she took out her phone and looked to be typing out a text and firing it off, smiling to herself. She seemed to interrupt herself then, perhaps trying to be discreet, she pocketed her phone and hid the secret smile from her friends. Jasper was always intrigued by a secret and felt sure she had one. Now he wanted to know more.

Jasper looked away quickly, avoiding the direct stare from the girl with the plaits. Once he knew she'd turned her back on him again, he raised his eyes. He watched them, intrigued. By now they'd passed him and headed up out of town, presumably to check in and unburden themselves of their substantial backpacks. They were definitely worth keeping his eyes on. He looked back towards the bus station but despite the milling crowds, nobody else caught his eye and he stood, ready to push on with work.

As the afternoon passed, Jaspers eyes kept dragging back to the road the four girls had disappeared up, they hadn't left his thoughts and now he hoped he would see them again.

***

Jasper had busily worked all day. As the afternoon wore away he headed to a small café further along the High Street to eat. Sitting and chewing, his mind drifted back to the four girls. Four very different girls and appeal in each of them. Once he'd finished eating, he went for a walk along the beach, wasting time really until the tourists began drifting down from hotels and holiday homes to enjoy the night life.

Later, he sat in the window of a small pub that overlooked the centre of town, confident that he'd see them again. It wasn't long before he did. Weaving down the road they'd departed on earlier, he suspected they were already drunk. They looked different in their evening clothes but still very much different from each other. Jasper watched them enter a pub on the opposite side of the road and sat back, happy to wait and see their next moves. He had strengths and weaknesses like anyone, but his patience was definitely a strength.

Over two hours passed before they emerged again, giggling into the street. Jasper watched as the four young women huddled together, talking and gesturing. The one with silky black hair kept gesturing behind her. Jasper wondered if she was trying to convince the others to go somewhere. The free-spirit and the one with plaits earlier both seemed to stand, wide-eyed as the one Jasper thought of as 'left out' was gesturing behind her and draping a hand across her forehead. Even from where he sat, Jasper did not believe what seemed to be a charade of illness. Eventually after much back-and-forth conversation and gesturing, three girls went one way and one the other. Jasper quickly swallowed the dregs of a coke he'd been nursing and following the girl that was now alone.

When she'd left her friends, she'd walked as if heading up the hill in the direction they'd come when the night started. She waited and once Jasper saw her friends turn out of site, his quarry also suddenly changed direction and dipped into a side street. Her dress bounced with each step she took along with her bobbed hair. She kept checking over her shoulder, but her eyes seemed to glide over Jasper. He wasn't who she was looking for.

As she turned into an alley, cutting through to the sea front she nearly bumped into another man. Jasper crept closer, pretending to use a pay phone on the corner. The man, awkward looking and clearly drunk draped an arm across Ria's shoulders and leaned in as if to kiss her. She pushed him away with two hands and Jasper heard her shout at him 'Back off Nathan, I'm not interested.'

Ria marched forward, intent on her destination and the man, Nathan, slunk towards Jasper. Before he was able to leave the alley, Jasper had stepped out from the phone box and into his path. Grabbing the collar of his crumpled shirt, Jasper thrust him, headfirst into the wall. Nathan, eyes wide and clearly startled, tried to stagger backwards, but Jasper did not let go. He glared at him, close to his face. 'You never touch her again.'

Jasper didn't so much speak the words as snarl them,

spit flying from his mouth and landing on the creature in front of him. Eventually, Jasper opened his hand, releasing Nathan and indicating with a lift of his chin that he should leave, and now.

Jasper stood rigid for a moment, breathing deep and smoothing his hair down, so it flopped next to his face. He smoothed his clothes and smiled, before walking on towards the sea.

When Jasper emerged from the alley, he saw Ria with her back turned towards the sea, leaning against the railing. Her eyes were scanning constantly, her hands brushing down the lower edges of her dress. Jasper assumed that meant that she was waiting for someone. He wondered who that could be.

After a few moments, she turned slightly, still leaning against the railing, but now her fingers dancing along the top rail, back and forth. Her eyes slowly lowered, and Jasper enjoyed being able to watch more freely, unafraid of her seeing him.

Her eyes slowly drifted up until, in one moment, her face and body language sprang into life, gravitating to a point outside of Jaspers field of vision. Her face suddenly danced with light, her body seemed somehow more graceful, more womanly.

In time with the change in her, Jasper felt the warmth from her too. He felt the corners of his lips gently turning up, his physical reaction, to her physical reaction.

At that point, a man stepped into Jasper's sight, in the path ahead of his target. His eyes sparkled and he looked as enchanted by this young woman as Jasper was. The look between them was electric. Jasper struggled to interpret it, they seemed to share knowledge of each other but still had the slight awkwardness of new acquaintances. They stepped slowly closer together until their hands touched, fingers lacing between fingers. Delicate touches slowly growing with confidence.

Throughout, their eyes never left each other. Some feeling within Jasper rose up like a serpent ready to strike. He hadn't yet chosen, how dare this man sweep in and try to interrupt his plans?

Jasper sunk back into the alley behind him and allowed his fingers to wrap around a green beer bottle, hurling it violently against the wall. The explosion of glass crashed through the quiet calm of the previously magical evening. Jasper hoped it would kill the mood, if nothing else.

Jasper walked, fast, head down, the pavement taking the brunt of his irritation. His heart pounded loud in his ears, overpowering normal thought and trying to free his raging fists from where he'd stowed them in his pockets.

It didn't feel like he'd pounded the streets for long. He'd skirted around the centre of town, wide circles until his breathing became level and he was able to be the smiling and pleasant man he usually presented to the world. When he finally felt in control again, hours had passed. He looked up and saw the back of a floral dress floating up the hill. Jasper hesitated a moment, it looked like Ria's dress, but he wasn't certain. Without thinking fully, he found himself racing up hill on a parallel street. Desperate to see her, an angry fire within also wanting to see him, the man she had been with. As he reached the top, beads of sweat prickled his forehead, he quickly swiped them away with the back of his hand and turned a corner onto a road that would intercept the road the floral dress had disappeared along.

As Jasper approached the junction, Ria crossed his path, alone. She glanced in his direction, looking contented and serine. He threw a casual but warm smile her way. She vaguely reciprocated before drifting on. Jasper felt a pull of rage deep down. She had barely noticed him.

Once they'd disappeared from sight, Ria too changed direction and shuffled into the shadows before ducking down a side street, leading towards the sea. As she turned in, she almost bumped straight into a young man they'd met previously, Ria thought his name was Nathan.

As she tried to pass, Nathan draped his arm across her shoulders, leaning in close, stinking of beer and sweat. 'Back off Nathan, I'm not interested'.

Ria spoke almost over her shoulders as she'd brushed him off and continued walking, not giving him a second thought. As she reached the end of the side street, and turned the corner, she thought she heard the angry tones of someone saying not to touch her again. She shrugged, these towns, when they were full of drunk tourists, were a minefield, and she generally relied on the tactic of *ignore and keep walking.*

She walked along the promenade until she was in the spot where she'd previously arranged to meet Marc. They'd chatted via letter for months and shared photos, so she knew what he looked like. They'd also chatted on the phone, so she felt quite comfortable meeting him, other than the butterflies doing laps in her stomach. That was excitement though. She was more excited than she remembered ever being for anything else. At home she did what she was told to keep her mum off her back. At school, she did what she had to in order to get the grades she needed and the perfect school record she needed. Even with her friends, she felt like she was walking a tight rope. She never really did what she wanted, just the easiest choice that she could vaguely get on board with. Like this holiday. She came because she could see Marc, but into the bundle, she'd ended up doing lots of other things she had no interest in. Shots and random snogs just didn't interest her at all.

She'd been looking down, introspective, when she felt eyes upon her. Looking up, she saw Marc striding towards her, a comfortable and warm smile on his face.

He was better looking in person, an energy radiated from him of kindness and sincerity. He kissed her on both cheeks which felt very mature.

They walked along the beach and talked and drank in the sight of each other, wonderfully here together in the flesh. Marc had only an hour or two before he had to get back to his companion for the trip. Before they parted, Marc leaned in and gave Ria the gentlest brush of his lips on hers. Not the ravaging, devouring kisses Olivia had every other minute, but gentle and sensual. They made plans to meet the following day and as they parted, Ria felt like she was floating home. She walked on autopilot, taking in nothing of her surroundings, her head full of images and scenarios involving Marc. She even found herself saying her own name, the way he pronounced it *Ri-ah*, it sounded much more exotic. She walked around for a while before her feet led her up the hill to their holiday cottage. Despite Marc heading back to spend time with his friend, he still texted with her back and forth all evening.

Finally, she crawled into bed, satisfied to have accomplished something just for her. She had been a pen pal with Marc for four years and had felt meeting him would be impossible until recently.

Ria had never really enjoyed the trashy romance novels that Callie and Olivia read, but now she was beginning to understand the appeal. Romance, love, boys, they'd never really been on her radar and now she had turned a light on to a whole part of her life and she knew there would be no going back. She hoped things could work with Marc, but even if they didn't, now she knew what she wanted.

***

When Molly, Olivia and Callie crept home in the early hours, Ria pretended to be asleep, a bucket sat next to her bed. 'She didn't even drink much' they'd giggled as they staggered out of clothes and into bed themselves.

When they finally settled and gentle snoring could be heard, Ria pulled her phone from under the duvet and tapped out a final reply before closing her eyes and this time, going straight into a happy and satisfied sleep.

6 – Molly – 09/06/1996

The heat of the day had worked its way through the cheap curtains making the room suffocating and sweaty. Molly tinkered in the kitchen making tea in mismatched mugs. When she returned to the bedroom with a tray, Olivia and Ria shuffled into sitting positions, but Callie kept her eyes steadfastly shut. They sat and cradled their drinks as they leaned against bunched up duvets. Molly could see the mascara streaked and smudged around her friends' bleary eyes and suspected she looked no different. They woke up slowly and dissected the night before.

Molly watched as Olivia expressed her outrage at Callie's choice of men while she sloshed tea on her mismatched pyjamas. 'The guy on the way home must have been fifty!'

Callie's suddenly flushed face contradicted her words as she smiled 'he was a very good kisser, thank you. I was a bit put off when he flopped his dick out but before that he was fine. Plus, he was an Aussie, so that's two continents so far, one to go!'

Tea was spluttered in all directions at this as the four of them collapsed in giggles.

The laughter eventually subsided 'showers or a swim in the sea before breakie?' Callie asked the group. Molly knew she'd make the decision before anyone else had even spoken and watched as she grabbed her swimsuit. She shouted 'Decision made!' Molly smiled at her friend. She was always such a rollercoaster of highs and lows. Feisty but kind, subdued and then way over the top.

***

The night before had been a heavy one and Molly enjoyed splashing in the chilly ocean, nursing a heavy head. She thought she saw secret smiles on her friends' lips, perhaps they were reflecting on the previous night's shenanigans. They soon wrapped themselves in sarongs and lounged outside a beach bar, awaiting breakfast butties and more tea.

While they were quietly awaiting their order, Simon and Stephen, two of the boys they'd met previously approached. They were each holding a tacky single red rose wrapped in plastic and each knelt chivalrously in front of their beau. Olivia gave Stephen a gentle kiss as she took her gift and Molly burst into giggles while watching before accepting hers.

'So, will you ladies be in Electro tonight? I heard it's better than the other clubs and owned by that bloke in Eastenders. Someone said he was there last night so we might see some celebs!' Stephen had taken Molly's hand as he spoke and finished with a kiss on her fingers as the lads backed away. 'Hope to see you there!' shouted Stephen over his shoulder, a twinkle in his eye as he snatched a final glance at Olivia

'They are gross' sneered Ria. Molly knew Ria hated the pleasure the others found in their conquests.

'I hope we don't see their friend Nathan later either, he tried to slime on me on the way home'. Ria admitted.

'Maybe we should head somewhere else, you know, avoid them.' Molly stammered.

She could see Ria was worried about seeing him later. She knew there'd be other guys in other clubs. There was certainly no shortage in this town.

Callie, who had clearly drifted onto another subject asked, 'Do you think they pay these charity workers much? It seems pretty easy, chatting to people on the street. I'm sure I could get people to give loads for a good cause.'

'That guy was here yesterday, I bet they put in the hours too.' added Ria, squinting in the bright light. With her pale skin, Molly thought a job standing in the sun was an unattractive option.

***

Knock off melon-flavoured liquor really was the work of the devil. The girls had swigged it in turns from the bottle and soon felt suitably tipsy. Molly was eager to go out so they could at least drink something more palatable.

They'd had two days of partying in Cornwall. Sneaky snogs, numerous unwanted gropes from drunk men, old enough to be their grandads and more booze than they'd had in the past twelve months combined. Molly had ordered fake IDs from a catalogue before the holiday. She'd had to get a cheque from her mum to pay for them and had told her it was for study aids. Molly cared a great deal about others but had a 'take it or leave it' attitude when it came to rules. As the girls drank, they reminisced about the previous night. They'd been to a dingy bar called Denny's just before going to the club. Molly was thankful Ria had already left, or she knew she'd have had a breakdown. The old and sweaty barman took their IDs and walked away. He disappeared out of sight for several minutes, during which the girls spoke in whispers, foreheads crinkled with worry in case the police had been called. The bar-tender returned, a good five minutes later, and Molly suspected he'd photo-copied their cards. He began serving the girls with no further problem. Molly was certain he could tell they were young, despite being caked in make-up. There was no hiding their baby faces, still rounded with puppy fat and naivete. If he could prove he'd checked the IDs though, all seemed to be well.

***

That night, they'd met up with the lads they'd met that morning but decided to ditch the club and head to the beach where they sat around a fire. Despite earlier reticence, Ria ended up sitting with Nathan, although she'd made it clear she was not interested in anything beyond talking. As the four girls and four boys passed a spliff around the fire and swigged from cans of beer the guys had brought, Molly noticed that Ria seemed to be loosening up and enjoying the party atmosphere. Despite Simon's efforts, Molly just wasn't in the mood. She just wanted to sit around the fire and chat and drink and smoke.

'Nathan, have you got a cut on your head? What happened?' Molly asked. From her current angle it was more pronounced than when she'd previously looked at him.

Nathan looked down, then sheepishly at Ria. He directed his answer towards Ria. 'Last night, after I saw you – sorry about that. A guy smashed my head against the wall and told me to leave you alone.'

Molly watched as Ria processed this. 'Why?' she finally blurted.

'Maybe someone's got a crush on you Ria' Molly teased.

Molly knew Ria felt left out sometimes. It was never her the men were after. It was never her that got the valentine's card or the rose.

As the evening progressed, Molly saw Nathan became more persistent with Ria, covering her mouth with his and her breasts with his awkward hands. He pushed her back into the sand.

Molly shouted across the sand, knowing that Ria would not be happy. As soon as Ria could free her mouth she screamed, loud and angry too. 'What are you doing? You know I'm not into you!'

Standing, Molly held her hand out to Ria, helping her to her feet. 'Callie, Liv, come on, it's time to go.'

Molly began walking, pulling Ria along behind her, as Callie and Olivia extricated themselves from their partners.

***

The walk home was quiet. Ria hadn't appeared too traumatised by the situation, but Molly certainly felt the momentary vulnerability. It was only when they were going to sleep, Molly heard a sniffle or two and slowly crept over. Ria was sobbing. Now she was safe in bed, the fear and helplessness hit her, and she was shaking uncontrollably.

Molly knew she was replaying what could have happened, especially if her friends hadn't been there. Molly curled herself up on the edge of the bed, holding her friend's hand tightly, a warm safe space between them. Eventually the two girls fell asleep. Molly's arm remained draped protectively over her friend throughout the night. Molly woke in the early hours and crawled back to her own bed, quickly drifting back to sleep.

***

Molly smacked at her alarm and sat up in the dark room. She quickly tugged on clothes that she'd left on her bed and stepped out to the kitchen where she'd left supplies. Filling a water gun she re-entered the bedroom. 'Wake up ladies!' she squealed.

When the anticipated reluctant grunts escaped from her three friends, Molly let rip, squirting each of them with water from a super soaker that she brandished like a machine gun.

Moments later Molly felt her knees buckle as Callie had thrown her body weigh at the back of her legs. Molly collapsed under the fragrant and angry form of Callie, pinned until Callie moved.

'What the hell Molly? Why are we awake at ... five in the morning?' Molly could only just hear Callie's words as her arm was pinned across her ear.

After multiple attempts to shift herself sideways, Molly rocked back and forth until Callie fell off her before answering. 'We need to go to the beach, I have something special planned. Quick, we don't have much time.'

***

In single file they skirted the rocky cliffs until they

opened out into a shallow cave. Ducking inside, they settled their bags on a dry rock and Molly shook off her shoes and set about rolling a joint. The four sat together, crossed-legged on the sand, passing the haze inducing cigarette between them. The light was just beginning to creep above the horizon, but the sun had not yet made an appearance.

'Sorry, I'm still rubbish at rolling' Molly said while dipping her head down. Her long hair creating a visual barrier around her face, guarding her insecurities and adding an air of mystery.

'Better than my efforts' Callie jumped to her feet grabbing her bag and another bottle of cheap booze, this time lemon-flavoured. She swigged, screwing her face up before handing it on to Olivia. Molly peeped out from behind her hair and watched as Olivia sat quietly, inhaling deeply from the cigarette and exhaling in a cloud of relaxation. Molly knew she struggled to relax, sometimes a joint was the only way. As the smoke billowed around her, Olivia swigged deeply from the bottle, her face switching through a series of expressions as she did. 'I suppose we won't get hungover if we just keep drinking.' Molly smiled at her friend, she was always willing to join any crazy plan they had.

Ria was happily chattering away and Molly watched her trying to start a small fire. Ria always had a lot to say but was not always in tune with the conversations around her. At present she was balancing the pros and cons of getting high, ending abruptly as Olivia held the spliff to Ria's lips. Shrugging she inhaled.

'Got to be better than that' she motioned towards the bottle of booze Olivia was still swigging. As she passed the spliff back to Molly, going full circle, they all relaxed into it. As Molly began to roll again, Callie brought out a small cassette player. As she depressed the play button the iconic sound of Slash's guitar filled the cave and echoed back at them. Callie began a wild moshy, dance, bouncing energetically, her slim frame and neat hair thrown gracefully in every direction. Before, Ria was up. She always loved to dance although potentially to more of a cheesy beat. She bopped and swayed, seemingly to her own tune but now much more mellow and enjoying herself. Glasses perched on her nose and hair in a messy ponytail, bare toes scrunching in the sandy floor.

Molly stood, sparking the next joint and swaying gently to a much slower tune than the others could hear. Olivia sat back leaning on her elbows, happily swigging and enjoying the music from her place. She never danced as much as the others, unless there was a man to grind up against, but seemed to enjoy the music from where she sat.

Molly knelt down, drawing her bag towards her, wincing at the scolding sun-burn on her shoulders and upper arms. Sucking deep on her spliff as analgesia, she continued to rifle through her bag, pulling free four slender wooden wands and four sparkling tiaras. She'd brought them with her from home. She'd had to pretend they were a prop for a play when her Mum asked about them. Molly danced around the other girls, crowning each of them and bowing deeply while she offered them their wands.

Next, she brought out four candles and some incense. 'Shall we get this show on the road?' she asked, handing out candles and incense to each of her friends.

'Yeaaahhhhhh' Molly screamed, zooming out of the cave and onto the wide sandy beach ahead of the others, spinning in circles, free as a bird. When they caught up, she was pacing about marking a large pentagram in the sand, placing her candle in a spot on one side. She then set about lighting incense and placing it in the centre of the star. Once she was ready, she looked up to the others, nodding for them to take their places. Callie and Olivia moved around but Ria hesitated. The others knew she'd been torn about this. Her family were Christian and would be unlikely to approve of such behaviour. Her indecision played across her face before she finally threw down her wand and tore the tiara off her head, throwing them into the pentagram and turning away 'I just can't', she shouted over her shoulder as she walked away.

Molly, Callie and Olivia shrugged and shuffled sideways, so they were evenly spread around the star before each raising their arms, wand in hand and whooping joyfully into the fresh morning air. They were anticipating Ria's departure and were unperturbed by it, leaving her discarded items where they fell. They'd chosen sunrise for this gathering and as the first of the sun's rays danced above the horizon, they glistened tantalisingly across the water. The three remaining friends began to chant. Molly had found the words in the old tome of her grandmother's that her mother had kept locked in a chest. Molly had been obsessed with it since she first cast her eyes over it.

By rising sun and night that fades
Friendships held fast, strong in spades
Woven wishes tied as knots
Bindings of fire in their cooking pot
Night has gone, now night shall pass
The magic hour, gone so fast
Away now fly those gone are lost
To the wind their souls shall be tossed.

Molly insisted that the description of the spell was a close binding of friendship. Once the chanting was over, they entered the pentagram, and Molly removed a long flowing scarf that had been draped around her neck. With arms held out, she bound them together and they repeated the words a second time before sitting at the centre of the star and finishing the bottle of lemon booze between them. Still tied to one another, Olivia began to lean and then topple, she brought the others with her until all three were a giggling mess of limbs strewn across the sand.

When the laughter faded, they lay for a while, still and peaceful and close. Molly felt the power in the pentagram and in the words spoken with her true friends. She knew there was more to it than the others would admit.

The sun had fully risen above the horizon and Molly lay on the sand, calm and content.

'Do you think we should go find Ria?' Callie whispered, an unusually gentle tone to her voice. Molly finally sat up and pulled at their binding. Once free of the binding, she took out her lighter and held it under the scarf until it caught, shrinking in the heat. Molly squealed, feeling like it was the perfect end to their ceremony. As the flame died, they walked away, arm in arm to find their friend, it felt wrong to be too long without her.

7 – Callie – 09/06/1996

Callie didn't believe in any of Molly's witchy rubbish, but she liked a laugh. She also liked pushing buttons and she knew Ria would hate the wands and the pentagram and all the rest. It had pleased her when Ria had done what she knew she'd do. She left them. Again.

Callie thought Ria had been nothing but boring all week, heading off early, not drinking much and not really joining in. It was like having an annoying big sister along for the holiday, one who had forgotten what fun was. It wasn't often that Callie allowed herself to soften and be more reflective, but she had been thinking about the holiday being the end of an era. The four of them had been friends since primary school and had never seemed to shake each other off. Callie thought that this might be it, the final hurrah before they drifted apart. Ria and Molly were likely going to university in the autumn, but Callie supposed that meant she'd still have Olivia. She almost felt pre-emptively lonely at the thought of their dysfunctional little friendship group no longer being her rock. Callie was good at playing the tough girl. It had been how she'd stopped bullies in the past and broke through the stereotypes people tried to force on her.

She'd lived in Oxfordshire her whole life, been born there, but people still asked where she was from. Which usually prompted her to respond with *where are you from you rancid little shit* or something similar. The aggressive tone usually shocked but then shut people up.

After 'witching' they met back up with Ria and had a pleasant breakfast at a little café where they were quickly becoming regulars.

'I think' Olivia began, looking longingly back toward the busy streets in the town 'I think I'll get my belly button pierced if there's somewhere here that can do it.'

Callie watched Molly literally bounce with glee. 'I'm in.

Me too! I was thinking about getting a tattoo, but I may just get both!' She had gone high pitched as she always did when excited.

'I would like a tatt and maybe the top of my ear pierced too' added Callie in her usual more morose way.

Ria said nothing and turned towards the sun. Callie knew she was avoiding any potential pressure that might be aimed in her direction, so she left her in peace to decide for herself. She'd had enough of trying to include someone who didn't want to be included.

***

Olivia sat frozen, eyes tightly shut. Callie knew that she was afraid that if she moved, the needle would stab her in the wrong place. The smell of disinfectant lay heavy in the air. Moments later, Olivia had a beautiful chrome ring in her navel and was exhaling gently. She seemed relieved it was over. Callie was watching and swallowing down her own nausea. Olivia had wanted her navel pierced ever since seeing a music video where a girl got one. Callie thought it looked good on her, so why not?

Molly sat carefully in the chair next, giggling and seemingly unaware as the needle went in. Callie felt her usual sickness rising up again and getting beyond her control. She glanced in one of the many mirrors and could see that her skin was practically translucent. As the heavily tattooed and bearded man had moved on to her and pierced her upper ear. In style true to herself, Callie staggered outside and vomited in the nearest gutter to the echoes of her friends teasing her amid giggles. She recovered quickly and stepped back inside.

Her moments of clarity after vomiting allowed Callie to notice how quiet Ria was. As the technician was finishing up with Callie, she watched, irritated but unsurprised when Ria announced she was going to look in the shop next door and marched away.

Callie and her two remaining friends now took turns to

get tattoos. Molly got a wonderful selection of tiny spiders, making a web from her collar bone. Olivia managed a small tree on her shoulder saying it represented *wisdom, of course* and Callie had a vine, wrapped neatly around her ankle. Olivia had to practically drag Callie out of the door before she requested anything else. Callie felt that a selection of tattoos would allow her to share her personality more clearly. Her friends seemed unconvinced. It took nearly an hour before they found Ria again, way down the street, exiting a dingy bar that certainly did not seem like her kind of place. 'I just needed the loo' she pre-empted before they could ask.

Callie paused for a moment, eyeing her friend. She had become a connoisseur in bullshit and Ria certainly stank of it. She decided not to press the issue, happy instead to enjoy their freedom. She would certainly be keeping a closer watch on her friend from now on.

***

Callie loved an Irish bar; they were always good fun with music and laughter. She felt like friendships were slowly falling away and couldn't bear the thought of the loneliness that might replace it. She hoped if nothing else, Olivia would still be there for her when the others moved on in their lives. With that in mind, while sat at their table in the window, she put on her best attempt at entertainment, hoping to keep her friends close. She told silly stories, joked and even ignored it each and every time Ria rolled her eyes or sneered at what she was saying. She was trying her best to keep their group together. Even if none of the others seemed to care as much as her. Particularly Ria who kept disappearing at every opportunity.

When they left the pub and were talking about their next destination, another pub or an early arrival at a club, shockingly, Ria decided to go home early again, feigning illness. Callie knew she wasn't ill. What was she doing?

Callie refused to react and as Ria walked away, she made an extra effort to engage Olivia and Molly in hilarity, purposely refusing to look back or allow a single thought of Ria Roe to enter her thoughts again.

Callie linked arms with her friends' arms, and they walked on down the street. Another pub, another drink and another opportunity for Callie to show them how much they needed her. They decided to skip the club and while they laced their way through the streets, Callie saw a familiar face. The charity worker they'd seen every day was still in the High Street. He'd removed his tabard but that didn't stop Callie. She dragged her friends along by their hands and approached, pulling her camera out of her handbag. 'Cosy up for a photo' Callie ordered.

Olivia and Molly draped an arm across each of the man's shoulders, tongues out, pulling a range of faces for the camera. 'Molly swap out for me'. Callie said, while manoeuvring Molly out of the photo, handing her the camera. 'I only have two shots left so make them good!' Callie spoke while replacing her and waving peace signs in front of her eyes.

Throughout this interaction, the man stood still, a shocked look on his face, mouth hanging slightly open. Callie laughed as they left, she loved to shock people and even more to document it.

They walked down the street, voices raised here and there above the melee of sounds. 'Stop,' Callie shrieked. 'I just heard an American accent.'

Callie had so far kissed a European and an Aussie and an American would complete the dare she'd been set for the week. Within minutes, Callie had left her friends behind and was eye to eye with a mousy haired American with a dusting of stubble. Callie had mulled whether to speak but instead she just looked at him and got gradually closer until they were lip locked. Moments later, Callie walked away without so much as a word or a backward glance.

8 – Jasper – 09/06/1996

During the bright, fresh morning heat, Jasper strolled through the High Street. Not working, just watching. It took a while before he found what he was looking for. He heard them before he saw them. Giggling and teasing the black-haired girl, who he now knew was called Callie. She was outside a piercing and tattoo shop, vomiting into the gutter. Once finished, she sucked in a deep breath of air before heading back inside. Jasper hovered in the street, amongst stalls selling tourist tat and inflatables. It wasn't long before Ria stepped backwards out of the tattoo shop, talking over her shoulder as she left. When she entered the main street, she looked back over her shoulder, clearly, in Jasper's mind, to ensure her friends weren't following her. He had a moment of hesitation, deciding whether to stop and wait to see what the three girls in the shop did, or whether to go after Ria.

He made his decision and casually joined the flow of strolling tourists, keeping enough distance between him and Ria to prevent suspicion.

Jasper watched as Ria approached a dimly lit pub. It was more of a local's boozer than one usually frequented by tourists, and he wondered why Ria had chosen it.

Ria's fingers were jiggling before she reached for the door; she seemed nervous. She reached out and pulled the door of the pub towards her and Jasper watched from outside as she entered. The windows were ornate with writing obscuring much of their surface. A perfect place to lean against a dusty sill and peer through the gaps. The man behind the bar stood polishing glasses with a dirty looking tea towel and Ria stood inside the door, her head turning from left to right as she scanned the room. She headed into a corner thankfully within sight of Jasper's station.

He watched as Ria shuffled across the bench seat,

withdrawing a small mirror from her bag. She didn't look like she wore much make-up, but she seemed to be streamlining and flattening her hair. She impatiently rapped her fingers on the table and endearingly made tiny houses by balancing beer mats. Impatient to see more, Jasper decided to be bold. He moved across to the door and strode in. Ria's head shot up and her eyes locked on him before they glazed in apparent disappointment. 'Alright if I use the loo mate? Trying to hydrate and the public loos are the other end of town'.

'Yeah, go for it. I've seen you putting the hours in,' the barman laughed. Jasper dlsappeared into the rear of the pub and used the questionable facilities.

When he'd finished and gone back to his spot outside, it was moments before he heard the squeak of the door and watched Ria's head spring to attention again. This time, her eyes lit up and she brushed aside the beermat houses she'd made without a thought.

A man joined Ria at the table, the same man she'd met before. He was full of kisses and hand gestures and life. Jasper sneered at the newcomer that had distracted his prize. The couple at the table leaned in towards each other over the narrow table, eyes locked and the world outside forgotten.

Ria didn't know Jasper but that didn't stop him feeling forgotten when her attention was so firmly fixed on someone else.

Jasper watched until he could bear it no longer and stomped away. He would refresh at home before heading out later.

***

Jasper occupied his usual spot by the bank. He had watched groups of young people coming and going. He generally worked in the daytime where there were more people and a greater chance of customers, but he had decided to stay later this day, hoping to see the group of girls that had caught his interest, out on the town. He had calmed down after what he'd observed in the morning and now felt ready to start again.

It didn't take long. At half past seven, he saw the four of them, tottering down the hill and onto the High Street. He enjoyed watching people and the dynamics when they were in groups. When these four girls walked, one was always sidelined. They walked close to each other, deep in conversation, arms sometimes linked, sometimes not, but their closeness didn't always extend to Ria, the more conservative one.

Now he'd learned her name, he enjoyed running it through his mind. Ria, Ria, Ria. Ria walked slightly behind and to the right of the other three girls. She often looked all around, scanning the crowd. What was she looking for? he wondered, or who? Perhaps the man from the bar earlier.

Jasper watched as the young women headed into an Irish bar, within his line of vision. This decided him. He would stay and wait until they came out, he just wanted to see more. He sauntered along the street until he was opposite the pub and able to see in through the large windows. He could see the girls, clustered around the end of the bar, then getting their drinks and moving to a table, thankfully close to the window.

Jasper couldn't hear them, but he enjoyed watching the fleeting expressions on their faces as they talked. Now he watched, it seemed to him that it was mostly Callie doing the talking. She seemed to be holding court, while the others chipped in when needed. The long-haired girl seemed to be wearing a mask. Laughing and giggling with the rest but then filled with sadness in the in-between moments. The other girl, who usually wore her hair in plaits but today looked like a mermaid with her crimped hair, seemed to jump at every word, a born follower. Despite being close, it seemed to Jasper that they were all wearing masks of one sort or another.

Ria seemed alert and engaged, but Jasper did see the odd sneer or eyeroll. It was clear she was not quite in sync with the others. With me though, she could be in sync with me. In her movements, he observed her to be decisive, there was no dithering with her, she knew what she wanted. The black-haired girl seemed very fond of gesturing with her hands. She had slim wrists and a certain grace in her movements that intrigued Jasper. He would like to touch those graceful hands.

As he watched, Ria got to her feet, gesturing to her friends and she then appeared in the front door of the pub. Withdrawing her phone from her pocket, she again scanned the street before jabbing away at her phone with her index finger, apparently texting someone. She stood then, phone out, staring at the screen, expression full of anticipation. After a minute or two, her face lit up, a smile slowly spreading. She slid the phone back into her pocket and rejoined her friends. Once she returned to the table, it was clear in her body language that she was now much more buoyed and alive. She no longer showed irritation at her friends and seemed to unwind and begin to enjoy herself.

Why though, could she not text someone in front of her friends?

Jasper had begun to take an interest in *girl four* as he'd referred to her in his head. The one that often wore plaits. As he watched she stood and grabbed her bag and appeared at the front door where she lit a cigarette and puffed gently. Her legs had a fragility to them and something propelled Jasper forward and before he'd really planned anything, he was smiling, eyes twinkling and fully turning on the charm for Olivia. She introduced herself and offered him a cigarette. He accepted it despite hating them, he wanted an excuse to talk to her. 'I know you can smoke inside, but my friend hates smoking so I came out here for a peaceful time.'

Olivia smiled and Jasper could feel she was beginning to flirt with him, her body language had softened and become more enticing. 'I'd better get back to my friends,' Olivia whispered conspiratorially while stomping on her cigarette butt. 'Nice to meet you....?'

'Jasper, I'm Jasper. Nice to meet you too.'

Olivia leaned in and kissed Jasper gently on the lips but seemed to change her mind halfway and leaned in further, practically eating him alive. Jasper responded of course, and moments later, she was gone, leaving him full of a mix of emotions bubbling up beneath his amiable exterior.

Jasper wiped his mouth on his sleeve as he walked back across the road. He would keep watching, he was still unsure which would be the best fit for him.

9 – Ria – 09/06/1996

Ria had again slipped away from her friends and strode straight to a bar at the other end of town. This bar was more up market than the places she'd previously met him. The waiters threw out snooty looks as often as breathing and the dark décor and mood lighting made Ria feel decidedly out of place. She spied her beau across the room and headed towards him, the sparkle of attraction in his eyes clear, even from a distance. The nervousness she'd felt at their first meeting had disappeared and she couldn't wait to see him.

He stood when Ria approached and she flung herself at him, her lips finding his. She felt most unlike herself. The man was Marc and Ria had been in touch with him for years. It was only now, on this holiday, she was finally able to meet him. She hadn't told her friends, she didn't want them to mock her or question her loyalty for ditching them. She hadn't expected to fall so hard so quickly, but she absolutely had.

Ria sat at the table, gazing at Marc, his olive skin and slightly curly brown hair looked exotic to her, but mostly, she appreciated the kind and open nature he possessed. He was so warm and positive in everything he said, it was like a whole part of the world she'd never known about had now erupted around her and she was basking in the glow of it. She had wanted to meet him of course, but she never imagined that it would lead to an actual love affair.

After a couple of drinks, the pair left together, becoming more brazen now. They walked gently towards the beach. 'I think I should just tell my friends about you. I don't really know now why I kept it secret all this time.'

'You must do what you wish, so long as they don't take you away from me.' Marc's French accent gently purred as he spoke, seducing her with every word.

'I got a dare this week, to go skinny dipping. Fancy it?'

Marc face creased in puzzlement 'Sorry, what is that?'

'Swimming. Naked swimming. Would you like to?'

Marc smiled warmly, his eyes twinkling their excitement. 'Let's go.'

The pair walked to the far side of the broad beach, in the near darkness. The lights twinkled from the promenade but only threw minimal light their way. When they were a few metres from the sea, Marc leaned in and gently kissed Ria, tugging at the straps of her summer dress, encouraging them to fall from her shoulders. Then, arms wrapped around her, he gently unzipped the back.

Ria held her dress tightly up and across her breasts. She felt comfortable with him, but this was still a big step for her. Marc peeling off his clothes until he was stood, naked and enthralling. 'I won't look, you come in when you are ready.' With that, he turned, and Ria watched as he slowly entered the gently sloshing water. Ria didn't hesitate. As soon as his back was turned, she dropped her clothes and followed. She was mesmerised by him and couldn't stop, even if she'd wanted to.

When the pair were shoulders deep, they splashed and laughed and eventually embraced. Lips meeting with growing levels of passion. As they paused, their heads stayed close and Ria curled into Marc's shoulder, wanting to be closer and enjoying the salty taste of his skin when she kissed it. 'We're going home in a couple of days. I wish we had longer.'

'Maybe you can visit me in Paris, I can visit you too at university perhaps? It's not that far. We can make it work.' Ria nodded and curled in closer to him, their legs entwined as they bobbed in the water. 'Come on' she teased and swam away from Marc in strong strokes before diving beneath the surface.

When Ria surfaced, Marc's face was filled with panic. Ria could see that he was breathing rapidly, his arms, now she was within reach, wrapped around her, almost taking her under. She could see that he could swim and couldn't quite understand the panic. He laid back and kicked his legs, aiming for shore, or at least to be able to touch the floor. Ria followed. Once their feet were able to firmly anchor themselves in the sand, he spoke. 'When you dived down, I just panicked. What would I do if you didn't reappear? I can swim, but I'm not a strong swimmer. I was just scared for a minute.'

'Well, I'm a strong swimmer so relax, nothing is going to happen.'

As she finished speaking, Ria gasped and disappeared beneath the water before exploding out again, laughing. Marc laughed along but still seemed nervous. Ria leant in and kissed him again, shocked at her own forwardness. She had never been like this with a man before. Never felt like she was enough without a mask on her

They tumbled out of the water, laughing again and more relaxed. Ria could feel her cheeks glowing as she walked out of the water, naked and more confident than she'd felt in her life. They dragged clothes onto damp skin, barely losing eye contact, then hugged close, trying to warm up as the night air cooled.

After a goodnight kiss, Ria walked up the hill alone. Contentment flowing through every part of her body and her brain. She could never quiet her mind but just then it seemed to breathe a sigh of calm, and she enjoyed it.

She arrived back at the cottage and despite thinking she should shower off the sea salt, she curled in bed straight away and began a stream of messaging with Marc. He was sporadic in his replies as she knew he would be. He had gone back to have drinks with his friend and couldn't be texting constantly. She lay in bed reflecting on how quickly her relationship with Marc had progressed and basking in the warmth of it.

10 – Jasper – 09/06/1996

When the girls left the Irish pub, Jasper watched Ria holding her tummy and looking sad before drifting away. She walked down the High Street, hugging her stomach theatrically and moving slowly and delicately until she rounded a corner. Then she upped her pace, her face broke out in a smile, and she marched straight into an upmarket wine bar.

Jasper had followed at a distance and once outside, peeled off his fluorescent vest and smoothed his hair down. He folded his vest neatly and tucked it into his back pocket where it peeped out, refusing to be hidden. Stepping slowly through the door, Jasper saw Ria embracing a man. The man had slightly curly hair and to Jasper's eye, style. Ria and the man gained their seats and began chatting, while draping hands together or on a knee. They seemed completely unable to stop touching each other.

Meanwhile at the bar, Jasper sat on a high stool 'Malbec please' he smiled at the young woman behind the bar before turning at ninety degrees to the bar where he could watch Ria discreetly, unnoticed.

The bar was nicer than most of the ones the young crowd tended to gravitate towards. Gentle music and candlelight pronounced romance from every direction. Ria gazed at the man with eyes sparkling magnetically. It was a privilege to see her so confident and playful, certainly a change to how she presented with her friends.

Jasper was still nursing his glass of wine, having watched Ria and her friend drink two glasses each. They rose from the table, hand in hand and sidled out of the bar. They seemed to be ensuring they didn't lose contact for a second. Jasper watched them leave and saw them head left, down towards the sea. He drained his glass and slid away, unseen, into the night.

The evening had cooled a little since he'd stepped inside and Jasper felt a small shiver run up his spine. He could just make out the shape of the couple ahead of him. They had paused, and it seemed a decision was being made. Ria was tugging gently at his arm, and he was trying to stand his ground. It seemed he too could not resist her charms and moments later, they shuffled down onto the beach and walked to the furthest section. Jasper stayed back, watching, waiting. He gasped when he saw the naked form of the man running into the sea, followed by Ria, exposed and exquisite. She seemed like a different woman form when she was with her friends, more confident and relaxed.

On the promenade, Jasper edged closer to one of the fixed telescopes dotted along the walkway. Sliding a coin into the slot he stood on tiptoes, looking towards the sea and watching Ria and her man. She seemed like a mermaid, dipping under the water every few minutes, laughter erupting from her as she splashed back to the surface. The way she looked at him, Jasper wished he was that man, that she would look at him that way.

Jasper watched as they swam and laughed. They clumsily dressed, tripping and leaning on each other, before slouching off. This time, he didn't follow.

Jasper walked back through town to his car, but when he was in the high street, he was suddenly accosted. Arms draped around his shoulders and the girl with the silky hair who screeched in his ear 'I'm Callie, this is Molly and Olivia.' Jasper nodded, trying to enjoy the chance meeting while his guts still writhed from witnessing Ria and the unknown man.

'I'm Jasper' he managed.

It was enough as Callie talked endlessly before taking a photo with him and her two friends before swapping in. Jasper felt uncomfortable and out of control. He did not like being taken by surprise and he certainly didn't like to have his photo taken by people he'd been watching. The last thing he needed was for them to be able to remember him. He wanted to blend into the background.

Jasper drove back to the farmhouse that he currently called home. After a brief snack, he walked straight through the house and out the back door, and over to the old barn. Within the barn he'd already found what he might need when he arrived, now he needed to make sure he was ready. Time was short and he needed to act, before something or someone got in the way.

11 – Callie – 10/06/1996

The evening began much as the other evenings had. The girls sat in their cottage eating cheap student food and pre-loading on some nasty spirits Callie had acquired, while dancing and laughing and teasing each other. Their faces took turns to screw up while they tried not to gag as the volatile gin fizz that they were swigging hit their throats. Callie rolled her eyes as she watched Ria dancing happily, having added lemonade to her gin. She would never just join in fully. Callie lined up shots almost as soon as Molly, Olivia and herself had finished the last ones. Eventually Olivia slumped on a chair. 'No more or I won't make it out the door!' she groaned.

Molly was a lightweight, but she was also good at powering through and as Callie poured, she would drink, despite the swiftly progressing lack of coordination in her limbs. Callie wouldn't stop, not until Molly admitted she was done. It was something of a tradition between the two. Who could keep at it the longest.

Callie ushered the girls from the house. She felt unable to relax and slow down, regardless of the situation. 'We'll go to Pirate bar and then the club should be opening. You gonna make it Molls?' Callie teased Molly who was currently shoeless and staggering down the hill, a bad sign at the start of the night.

'I might go for a coke in the pub, then I'll be fine.' Molly focused intensely when uttering these words and seemed determined to keep going.

'I did offer you a mixer' Ria slid in. Callie knew she was attempting humour, but it came across as somewhat snidey, she rolled her eyes and made no reply.

As they approached the centre, Molly plonked herself on a low wall and replaced her shoes. She paused for a moment, breathing deep and hitching a cool and confident smile onto her face, before standing and doing a very good impression of a sober person.

They entered Pirate Bar, the bouncers merely glancing at them and ushering them through. It was dark and the air was sticky, drenched in sweat. The girls edged their way to the bar, with Callie at the front who ordered four tequila shots and four vodka, lime and sodas. The tequila was on sale, one pound per shot and Callie couldn't resist.

Despite her drinking as much or more than her friends, the alcohol didn't seem to affect Callie as much. She was taller but also seemed to have a higher tolerance than the others.

Callie led the group through the sweaty crowd to a high table where they could stand and rest their drinks, eyeing the other customers and looking for potential conquests.

'Watch out, there's that guy that keeps trying to sign us up to pay money to his charity. Steer clear or he'll have signed you up before you know it.' Callie was good at recognising people and he'd been on the streets all week. She had to give it to him, he did work hard. Olivia glanced then looked at her feet, Molly looked like she was struggling to focus on anything, and Ria was looking in the opposite direction, though what she was looking for, Callie couldn't tell.

Callie continued surveying the crowd, and when she looked across the bar to where a pole was positioned, she blinked to check her vision before a roar of laughter escaped her. Olivia had somehow darted over and was swinging herself round the pole and enticing a handsome young man with a ponytail to join her. Callie hadn't even seen Olivia leave the table. After watching Olivia get slowly closer to her target and getting him to dance on the pole too, Callie eventually jumped to her feet, 'time for the club'. She grabbed Olivia's hand and dragged her away as Olivia blew a kiss to her friend.

***

Callie watched, eyes narrowed against the smoky air,

as Ria disappeared out of the swinging doors of the club. Sneaking home early again she thought, shaking her head at her friend's lack of commitment to merry making. Callie kept her hand clasped around her glass as her eyes scanned the rest of the room. Olivia was grinding on the dancefloor with a young ginger haired man to the sounds of Edwyn Collins singing about 'a girl like you'. Her gaze bored into her quarry, oblivious to the rest of the room. Molly was nowhere in sight, Callie assumed she was probably hooking up with someone in a corner somewhere.

The dancefloor was interspersed with pillars and as Callie watched, a tall man with floppy hair leaned against one, his gaze scanning the dancers. A young woman with curly brown hair, who Callie would guess was younger than her, sipped from a tumbler before placing it on a shelf that laced round the nearest column. The man edged closer, his arm draped across the shelf. Callie watched, disgusted as he dropped something in the girl's drink, but then his eyes raised and met hers. Callie was marching towards him in seconds. He slunk sideways and disappeared into the crowd. Callie grabbed the spiked drink and tried to take it to the nearest bouncer to warn him but before she could take more than a step, she was yanked backwards, her hair tightly grasped by the young curly haired girl she'd saved from God knows what. She was on the floor before she could react, the drink snatched back and flung in her face. 'If you want it so bad, here!' The curly haired girl screamed in her face before turning and stomping away.

Callie picked herself up, looking around for the man who tried to spike the drink, but he was nowhere to be seen. Frustrated, she headed towards Olivia, grabbing her hand and yanking her away. Callie wanted to go home. She knew Ria was gone but had no idea where Molly was. She at least wanted to stick together with

Olivia.

Olivia didn't protest when Callie dragged her away. Callie knew Olivia would always be submissive to her and she relished that. Callie and Olivia marched up the hill to the cottage, avoiding piles of vomit and drunken lads roaming the streets. The smells of kebab shops left their drunken bellies rumbling but Callie was insistent on heading straight home. Halfway up the hill, Callie squatted down briefly, picking up something from the path in front of her. The streetlights reflected warm orange light from the silver in her hand, a necklace. As Callie looked closer, she fancied that she recognised it. 'This is Ria's necklace.' Callie observed, holding it up to her friend.

'Looks like it' Olivia confirmed, pulling two lollipops from her pocket that she'd taken from the toilet attendant earlier, clearly not too concerned about the necklace. They enjoyed the sugar hit as they headed home.

The door to the cottage was locked and the place was still cloaked in darkness. 'Ria left a while before us' Callie commented. The darkness unnerving her as Ria would normally have left a light on.

As Olivia bent to grab the key from under the plant pot, Callie saw a shadow move a few houses down and felt certain she could hear soft, careful footsteps. Deliberately quiet footsteps. Callie was usually the cavalier of the group but something, some sixth sense told her she needed to get inside quick. In the quietest yet most commanding voice she could muster she muttered to Olivia 'Get the door open and get in quick.'

As Olivia pushed the door open, Callie was close on her heels, hurrying her forward until her foot snagged and she fell toward the smattering of sand that had gathered on the hallway floor throughout the week. Callie didn't even check on her friend, she turned and slammed the door, locking it and drawing the curtain over it. She then darted about in the dark, she didn't want lights to cause reflections and stop her seeing outside. She looked initially from the kitchen window. The view directly out was clear, but she couldn't see sideways at all due to the low walls and hedges blocking her view. Callie darted up the stairs without pausing and stood gazing out, scanning the street. A shadow at the far end was slowly drifting away. She couldn't see enough in the blackness, but it looked like the figure of a person, dressed in black and clinging to the shadows of the street.

As Callie's breath began to level out, her head snapped sideways as she heard a scraping sound from the bedroom. She knew it couldn't have been Ria or Molly as they would have brought the key in. Her nerves jangling through her body, she tried to stay strong, that was always her role, to be the strong one. The vacuum sat lifeless, it's smiling face taunting her. Slowly Callie removed the pole from the hand attachment and lifted it until it was level with her shoulders, ready to swing if needed.

The sound persisted, no rhythm she could discern. With the pole in her right hand, Callie hesitantly switched the light on with her left, expecting someone to lunge at her any second.

When nothing was forthcoming, Callie slowly stepped forward, braced for an intruder and ready to knock his block off.

12 – Olivia – 10/06/1996

Callie always had to push. She always pushed and Olivia always let her. Olivia had drunk every shot put in front of her, but it was never enough, Callie always pushed for more. Eventually Olivia had reached her limit. 'No more or I won't make it out the door!' she groaned.

Callie didn't seem to care, she carried on drinking with Molly. Olivia felt the blood rush to her face and chest. She could feel it pumping through her, the panic rising as it always did when she said no. She knew Callie was not going to do anything, that there'd be no consequences, but that wasn't what she'd learnt in other situations and her body just reacted.

Standing up, Olivia shook out her limbs and stepped into the kitchen, pouring a glass of water and sipping it. She desperately wanted to splash water on her face but didn't want to have to re-do her make-up. Eventually, she levelled her emotions and rejoined the group. She wondered why Ria could push back against her friends, but she found it so hard. She craved the cocoon of their pleasure. When they were happy with her, she felt happy.

***

They entered the first bar and gathered around a table, Olivia saw her favourite feature of any pub or club. Ria was looking away, Molly was hammered, and Callie was scouting for talent. Without a word, Olivia slipped away. The music was loud, and George Michael's 'Fast love' couldn't have been a more appropriate song for Olivia as she gripped the pole and began swinging herself round it. Some men standing close gave a hearty round of applause which gave Olivia the boost she needed and only egged her on to dance ever more provocatively and entice a handsome long-haired man to join her.

Just as she felt she was settling into her rhythm, Callie grabbed her hand and she was pulled away, blowing kisses as she retreated.

***

When they hit the club, Olivia had no interest in anything other than dancing and finding someone to worship her for the evening. Callie had slunk over to the bar, though how she could even begin to drink more was beyond Olivia's comprehension. She'd seen Molly slumped in a booth alone, not long after they entered. She hoped she'd sober up a bit soon and join her in her quest for adoration. Ria, she was not surprised to see, had left early again. Olivia was almost tempted to follow her, wondering what she was doing each night she disappeared but then she felt a hand around her waist and began to sway. In moments she was throwing out her best moves and had forgotten her friends for the time being.

It felt to Olivia lately, that whenever she was getting going and enjoying her night, Callie seemed to drag her away. She seemed independent but Olivia began to wonder whether she was jealous. Jealous that Olivia was the object of desire for once. The centre of attention rather than Callie for a change.

When Olivia was dancing and hitting it off with a man, she felt alive. She found herself relaxing in a way she never normally could. Out in the streets she was always looking around, waiting for something to happen, but when she locked eyes with someone, she always felt somehow safe, protected. She wasn't naïve to the risks posed by men she hooked up with, not by a long way. She just knew that sometimes, the worst danger wasn't from strangers. When she looked around in the street, it wasn't logic that moved her, it was repetition. At home, in the quiet Oxfordshire town, her stepdad had eyes everywhere. Avoiding his spies was a hard habit to break.

As with every pub or club so far, it was Callie that decided when it was time to go. Olivia had spent the evening dancing and feeling great. Until Callie dragged her away again. Callie had an irritated look on her face and Olivia just smiled and played along. She didn't question why Callie needed to leave, she just went with it, she'd never win with Callie anyway.

Callie was on a mission, marching fast up the hill, her long legs making Olivia skip to keep up. Olivia felt it, as she was walking. The *impossible to describe how she knew* fact that she was being watched. Although fairly drunk, Olivia still felt able to scan the streets in each direction, still very much aware of her surroundings. Her impairment from alcohol dropped significantly as she felt the prickling of fear crawling up her arms as goose bumps. She could see nobody except some drunk lads that were oblivious to their presence.

Callie squatted suddenly and picked up something sparkling that she thought was Ria's necklace. Olivia had the feeling of something scary lurking that she didn't want to look at, like a child afraid to look under the bed. Instead, she pulled out a pair of lollypops she'd stashed in her pocket earlier and hoped the sugar hit would allow her to regain her rationality. Nobody was following them, nobody was watching them. Her stepdad was miles away and she'd consciously told him they were holidaying in a different town. She was safe and was constantly trying to remind herself of that fact.

She kept seeing creeping shadows and knew she was allowing her imagination to run wild, the quiet footsteps echoing through the now silent streets were in her mind and she refused to give in to it.

When they reached the cottage and found it still locked, Olivia was still doing all she could not to allow any negative thoughts in. When the key was still under the mat, Callie muttered something about Ria leaving before them, but Olivia just shrugged and picked up the key.

She was surprised when Callie suddenly seemed on alert and ordered her to open the door quickly. She did and, in the process, face planted onto the hall floor. Her knees scratched by the sand that had gathered in the hallway over the course of the week. Callie shut the door and raced around the house. Olivia lay face down on the floor, confused by her friend's suddenly strange behaviour and unsure what to make of it. Slowly, Olivia began to raise herself off the floor, just as Callie raced up the stairs. Olivia walked through to the living room and despite ignoring signs so far, something stopped her in her tracks. Something felt off, she wasn't sure what but crept up the stairs towards Callie. As her head peeped above the landing floor, she saw Callie poised with the hoover pole outside the bedroom door.

13 – Molly – 10/06/1996

Molly sat on the floor in the back of the club. She'd crawled away from the table she'd sat at alone, after vomiting beneath it. She had been unable to find the impetus to stand but had desperately tried to distance herself. Not wanting to get kicked out again, she sat propped against the wall, her shoes and bag cradled in her lap, her vision spinning wildly and worsening with every pulse of the lights.

As she sat, staring intently at a stain in the carpet, a shadow fell across her. Looking up, the silhouette of a man stood over her. 'May I?'

The man sat down beside Molly, a little too close but with a friendly smile on his face and proffering a glass of water. 'You look like you need this? How about you have a drink and then I'll take you downstairs for a smoke and some fresh air and you'll be ready to get back to the dancing?'

Molly took the drink, gladly gulping down the cool liquid and reaching into her purse for some tobacco to roll. 'I'm Molly' she smiled, giving a sidelong glance at her rescuer.

'Tom, here, let me roll that for you.'

Taking her tobacco tin, he slowly laid out the paper and loaded it for rolling, adding a home-made roach of rolled up card, prepared by Molly. Then, when running his tongue along the paper's edge to seal it, he looked at Molly from under his floppy hair. She felt drawn but also pushed down the nervous feeling as a shiver ran up her spine.

Once finished, Tom stood, leaning back down he took Molly's hand and pulled her up, before draping her arm around him. They slipped out of the club together, ensuring their hands were stamped before they left, with a barely decipherable smear of green ink.

14 – Ria – 10/06/1996

Ria curled into herself, the club was jammed wall to wall, and the smell of sweat laced the air. They'd arrived about an hour ago and ordered shots as the cheapest way to keep their buzz going. Ria could already feel her hair beginning to frizz at the humidity caused by so many clammy bodies. Olivia was busy grinding on the dancefloor with some less than appealing and grandfatherly-aged men. Molly sat in a booth, drunk, her head nodding at intervals. Callie was leaning on the bar, watching it all and she seemed to be deciding how to cause carnage next.

Ria knew that Marc was busy this evening. He had to see some relatives that lived in the area, so there was no real reason for Ria to sneak off early. When it came to it though, this holiday had made her realise that she just didn't like going clubbing. The pubs before were ok, with conversation and companionship, but as soon as they hit the clubs, everyone went crazy. If Olivia hadn't stuck her tongue down some unsuspecting man's throat within five minutes, she'd feel defeated.

'I'm not feeling great, I'm going to head home.'

Callie rolled her eyes in response. 'You won't turn into a pumpkin you know. Staying out past midnight won't kill you!'

Callie tried to play it as humorous, an insincere smile briefly showing on her lips, but Ria knew she was losing patience with her bailing on them all week. Callie always talked to Ria like she was a wet blanket smothering their never-ending fun.

Ria smiled through Callie's snarky comments, she was used to them. She walked away across the sticky carpet to the stairs. She dodged couples who really ought to have found a room elsewhere and avoided glasses left randomly on some of the steps.

Once outside, Ria sighed. She didn't want to be clubbing with her friends, but she didn't really want an early night either. What she wanted was Marc and nothing else would be enough until she saw him again. She thought he'd have at least texted her by now. The kebab shop was quiet, the hordes of drunken youths were still busy partying and had not yet descended on the eatery. Ria ordered a portion of chips and curry sauce and walked slowly along the beach, enjoying the burn of excess vinegar with each mouthful.

This holiday had changed Ria. She had experienced, even if only in small doses, the kind of happiness with Marc she'd never thought possible. Her parents had a functional marriage, but they never seemed to glow with love as Ria had done lately. Now she knew it was possible, she certainly wouldn't be able to settle for anything less.

Going back to her old life would now feel near intolerable. She still wanted to prove herself. She was determined to get into Oxford and was extremely driven, but she now understood it as one part of her life, and not her only source of motivation.

Ria nibbled her kebab shop chips, dunking generously in the pot of curry sauce she'd tucked into the soggy chip bag. She looked up at the skies and despite the town lights, she could see stars and feel the universe expanding before her.

The hill to their cottage rose before her and Ria meandered up, pausing often to look back and downwards towards the town. She had tried so hard in recent years to find a place for herself, to slot herself into friendship groups and assimilate. Now she finally felt the weight of expectation lift. She just needed to be her; the right people would find her eventually. She still cared greatly for the three friends she was on holiday with, but as they'd grown it became increasingly apparent that they were due to tread very different paths.

As Ria glanced again behind her, she kept walking forward. She gasped as she bumped into someone emerging from a side road. The curry sauce dribbled down onto her chest and onto the top of her dress. 'Gosh, I'm so sorry, I was distracted by the little cat over there and wasn't paying attention.' The man's eyes twinkled with kindness as he spoke.

He was familiar to Ria, they'd spoken earlier in the week, and she'd seen him around the town too. 'It's ok, I was distracted too.'

'I was just out for some air. Is your top going to be ok?'

'It'll be fine. You have a good evening.'

Ria had taken a napkin when she'd ordered food and began to use it to swipe at her top, flicking the excess sauce off. Her finger snagged and her necklace dropped to the floor. Ria shook her head, feeling calamitous. She gently placed her chips on the wall next to the path and knelt down to collect her necklace, hoping it wouldn't be damaged.

PART TWO

15 – Jasper – 10/06/1996

Jasper had been in the club watching the girls. All of them. He felt somewhat possessive of all four, but he would only have one. Tonight at least. The mermaid haired nervous one was dancing wildly. The free spirit sat alone. Ria had a brief exchange with the leader, Callie. Something about her made him feel angry every time he saw her. There was something a little too self-assured about her. Jasper watched as after speaking to Callie, Ria left the club. Jasper slipped quietly out after her, his decision had been made.

He watched Ria, there was something hesitant about her, she seemed to walk without any particular intention until she stopped and bought some chips and then turned, heading up the hill to where he knew their accommodation was situated. Jasper headed up a neighbouring street that ran parallel until he turned and was ready to intercept her path. His car was where he'd left it, at a junction on the way up the hill, knowing they would walk back this way. He peered through bushes at the corner, keeping himself hidden but watching for Ria to appear as she meandered slowly up the hill.

Jasper leant on the wall and peered through bushes, waiting to see the form of Ria, wandering up the hill. As she approached the corner, she glanced backwards, and Jasper took the moment as his own. He stepped out and into her path, colliding in an explosion of curry sauce. 'Gosh, I'm so sorry, I was distracted by the little cat over there and wasn't paying attention.' He said, smiling with all the innocence he could muster.

'It's ok, I was distracted too.' She said, and she seemed distracted still, this time by the sauce that has spattered across her top.

'I was just out for some air. Is your top going to be ok?' Jasper said this, shaping his face into a hopeful expression.

'It'll be fine. You have a good evening.'

At that, Ria turned, placed her chips on the wall and then knelt down. Jasper could feel the hard plastic in his hand, he didn't know why Ria was kneeling, but he took the opportunity and leaned over her, jabbing quickly before pocketing the needle. She looked up at him, confusion and fear etched in her expression, but her body didn't move. She had frozen, Jasper presumed from fear. He hoped she would not recover before the ketamine kicked in. Ria slowly rose to her feet, her eyes boring into Jasper's, horror seeping from every pore.

Just as she reached her feet, she stumbled forward, her muscles relaxing as she collapsed into Jasper's arms. He hugged her tight, enjoying the closeness and the sweet smell of her, burying his face in her hair. He knew to any observers, they would look like a couple in love. He hugged her close and pulled her arm around his waist and the other around his back.

The injecting had thankfully been easy enough, but getting Ria into the car had proved more difficult than he'd anticipated. She was a dead weight in his arms. By the time he'd clipped her seatbelt, Jasper was breathless and patched with sweat. He drove through the quiet streets with his window down, he couldn't afford a misstep.

His mind raced with both possibilities and catastrophes that loomed in wait for him. His previous failure was due to him focusing too hard. All his attention on dear Angela and none on the situation outside of the four walls of the house. That invited trouble and, in the end, Angela had to go. This time he knew he must keep his eyes trained on the full picture. Glancing sideways, he smiled gently, it would be tough to focus on anything but her. He had thought of taking her friend first, Olivia, she had a beautiful awkwardness about her which drew him in but in the end, something about Ria Roe was truly unique. She had a boyfriend which Jasper knew he could take advantage of.

The drive up to the farmhouse felt painfully slow and left Jasper a mess of adrenaline and nervous energy. When he pulled into the driveway, he stepped out and inhaled deep breaths, trying to regain his equilibrium and focus.

Jasper unlocked the door and headed inside, opening doors so that he could carry Ria in more easily. Once ready, he took a long drink of water and then headed back out to his sleeping muse. He opened her door, unclasped her seatbelt and took one arm, slowly leaning her forward and then hitching her into a fireman's lift, high on his shoulder. Again, her closeness, pressed against him encouraged a warm feeling within him.

He found her easier to carry now that he'd lifted her properly. He edged past the piles of boxes he'd stacked in the hallway and stepped down slowly into the basement. It was a small space, and he hoped she would not need to be down there long. He gently lowered her onto the metal framed camp bed he'd erected earlier. He crouched next to her and gently stroked her hair, brushing it off her face. His eyes felt full of tenderness and his touch was gentle, but it didn't take long for Ria to begin to stir. Jasper had decided he wanted her to wake up and get any tears and anger out of the way before he entered. A bottle of water sat on the floor next to the fold-out bed. He'd also left a bucket at the far end of the room; he figured she'd find it when she needed it.

Jasper stepped gently backwards and withdrew from the room to the sound of gentle breathing, intermittently interrupted by a snuffling sound as Ria tried to wake up. He clicked the lock behind him and sat on one of the boxes. He stacked them in the hall earlier to allow the basement to be completely empty.

Jasper listened as the sounds slowly grew until a moan slowly turned into a scream. Jasper could hear from the sounds of the creaking bed that Ria had now got to her feet. The steps raced towards the door and after the handle was tried and found locked, the fists hammered on the door until eventually she must have tired. Jasper could hear the scrape down the door and imagined her slumped on the other side. He lifted his hand, placing it gently and silently on the door, hoping to impart some comfort.

Several minutes later he heard Ria moving back down the steps and lots of banging and crashing and frustrated shouting. Once she's over the shock, it'll be fine. Jasper churned over his thoughts in time with the frustration emanating from the basement. He would need to keep her in line, and he knew how, he just hoped it wouldn't tip her the wrong way. He couldn't deal with another rebellion.

Jasper sat silently against the door for several minutes before finally moving off. He locked the front door and got back into his car. There were other loose ends he needed to tie up before the night was over.

***

Hovering in the shadows, Jasper stuck to the darkness, aware of Callie's turned head and her eyes scanning the street. The experience had been a closer call than he'd expected or wanted. It was done though, and he hadn't actually been seen. He hoped they wouldn't notice a thing.

The drive back to the farm was uneventful and Jasper felt himself slowly relaxing. He'd done it. When he got back, all was quiet. He paused, ear to the basement door and listened. There were gentle sounds of bare feet on a solid floor, pacing back and forth. Satisfied, Jasper moved on to make and eat dinner. He played music in the kitchen, loud enough to dull his over-stimulated mind and the sporadic shouts that occasionally arose from beneath his feet. He guessed she'd heard his return. By the time he ate it was the middle of the night, but he felt calmer and more himself again. He turned the music off and took a torch from the worktop and stepped out of the back door into the pitch darkness.

Up on the farm, there was no light, and the darkness felt all encompassing. His torch beam danced across the grass until it found his destination, the barn. He marched forward and unbarred the door. When he entered, he switched on the harsh overhead lights and could hear the quiet breathing beneath him. He was awake, Jasper was certain of that, but like a wily animal, he was holding back, waiting to see what he was dealing with before he made any moves.

16 – Molly – 11/06/1996

Molly woke feeling confused and detached. She staggered to her feet and moved away, lulled by the background pulse of the ocean and heading towards it.

When she reached the beach, she headed to the side to where she knew she would find an overhang of rock. She sat in the dark, slight twinkles reflected from the water, trying to sober up. Eventually she slumped and fell into a deep sleep, undisturbed by anyone in her solitude.

***

When Molly woke again, grains of sand from her cheek had found their way into her mascara caked lashes. Blinking away the sand and the sleep, Molly hauled herself back to a sitting position, the aching in her whole body surprised her. Her long skirt was hitched up enough to expose an enormous red and black bruise that blossomed on her shin. The nails of her toes were jagged with the polish chipped. She did not recall what Tom did when she lost consciousness and had no recollection of where she'd obtained these injuries. She had a flash of memory where she'd launched herself at Tom and knew they'd been very hot and heavy, but that was all she could recall. She groaned at how forward she could be when drunk but couldn't shake the sense that she was missing something. She stood and moved deeper into the overhang and squatted to relieve herself, noticing that her underwear was missing. A stinging pain shot through her as she did. She inhaled deeply and pinned that thought to the back of her mind, she would deal with that later when her brain felt clearer. She finished urinating and walked out of the cavern, across the sand and began to head home. The sun was well above the horizon, and the early dippers were splashing in the sea, laughter ringing in the air and the smell of sausage and bacon drifting towards her. Molly felt confused and thick headed as she walked, struggling to attach herself to reality. She ordered a bacon butty to take away from the beach café, hoping it would help her gain some clarity of thought. She nibbled as she shuffled up the hill to the cottage. Shards of panic began to pierce her at the thought of her friends worrying about where she'd been. She half expected a police car to be sat outside when she arrived. As the cottage came into sight, all was quiet, the curtains drawn. She crept through the front door and as she tip-toed into the bedroom she could hear gentle snores within. Two of her friends were sound asleep in their beds, Ria was not. It was 9am already and she suspected Ria had gone out for an early walk, she often went out early at home when she couldn't sleep.

Molly's insides sunk in disappointment as she realised that anything could have happened to her and nobody was even worried. She climbed into bed, the quiet voice inside her desperately trying to tell her that something *had* happened, but Molly closed her mind to it. She did not want to remember anything or think about anything at present.

Laying back on her pillows, her whole body ached, her eyelids were heavy. The sound of her friends' gentle snoring would normally lull her to sleep in seconds, but she lay with eyes open and her mind resolutely still, determined not to think about the last few hours. She could feel the whirling of memories behind a veil, and it took everything she had to keep the thoughts from surfacing.

After a couple of hours of staring at the grain of the wood that surrounded the upper bunk bed she lay on, the fidgeting of her friends told Molly they would be rising soon. With sleep still evading her, she slipped out of the room and doused herself in the shower until Callie's hammering on the door forced her to come out. The night had been washed down the drain and she hoped that she could now move on, ignoring the events of the night before. If she was honest, she knew what had happened. She had no memory, but her body had told her the story of the evening. She had no intention of burdening her friends with what she thought had happened. She intended to draw a line and as she stepped out of the bathroom, she pasted a smile on her tired face and pulled her towel up high to her neck to cover the marks she'd discovered on her breast.

Walking back into the bedroom, Molly threw on some loose clothes as Olivia slowly dragged herself out of bed and Callie exited the bathroom with a seemingly amazing lack of hangover of any kind. 'Has Ria gone out early again?' Molly asked, still stung by the lack of awareness that she'd been out all night.

'She wasn't here when we got back. I've not heard her come in. She's definitely been home though, the window in the bedroom had been left open. She's obviously up to no good'. Callie rubbed her hands together, clearly anticipating some sort of juicy gossip to come.

Despite feeling disgruntled that nobody had worried about her, Molly's heart rate jumped 'You know she wouldn't just stay out. You know that. Have you called her?'

Callie shook her head, she seemed unconcerned, and Molly tried calling her friend. 'Straight to voicemail. I don't like this, it's not like her. When did you guys last see her, I really can't remember.'

'I saw her leaving around eleven I think,' said Olivia. She scrunched up her face and Molly thought that she was still feeling the effects of a heavy night.

'Yeah, that's right' confirmed Callie 'I teased her about the early hour as she left. She said she was coming home. Perhaps we should have been worried, I wasn't really thinking.'

After half an hour of back and forth and various

scenarios that could potentially have played out, Molly reached for her phone and dialled the police. Her phone was slippery in her sweaty hands as she made the phone call for Ria that nobody had made for her.

It took several hours of pacing and wondering before a police officer hammered on the door. Molly gave the place a final glance, dropping a beach towel over the traffic cone she'd acquired. They'd tidied away the alcohol and tobacco tins while they waited; satisfied nothing had been missed she pulled the door open. Her hollow face, drained from lack of sleep, looked young and scared as she glanced in the hall mirror before greeting the tall police officer and leading him into the living room.

The officer's eyes danced across every surface and each of their faces in turn, before he finally settled and sat down. 'Right, from the start, tell me what has happened to your friend.' After speaking, he looked expectantly from one girl to the other, a mild expression on his face, inviting confidence.

Molly finally began, when she realised her friends were waiting for her to take the lead. 'Our friend, Ria Roe, she left the club before us last night and she hasn't come home. Well, she may have been home, but she wasn't home when we got back, and we haven't seen her since. It's extremely out of character for her, she's the one who leaves nights out early, the one who brings homework on holiday. She wouldn't have stayed out without telling us. Absolutely not. Never.'

Molly nodded as she finished, feeling satisfied she'd made her point and hoping nobody would add *like you* in reference to her staying out all night. If she still wasn't back, would they even be worried yet, or just think she had stayed out?

The police officer scribbled in his notebook and asked a series of questions about Ria's background and movements over the course of the holiday. Molly sat back a little and nudged Callie to take the lead. She felt exhausted and she could feel the bubbling of emotions just below the surface. If she couldn't keep her mouth shut for a while in silence, she felt the wrong words might just erupt out of her. An uncontrolled mix of bitter frustration and rage. She had decided she did not wish to speak to the police about her own suspected violation, and she was set on that decision, but it didn't make it easy while sat talking to a police officer.

Callie took the hint and Molly breathed deeply and listened to Callie chirp on about Ria's habits and usual behaviour. 'She is a bit of a square to be honest. She is my mate, she knows I'd say that too.'

The police officer, PC Davies nodded seriously before rising to his feet. 'Where is all her stuff? I need to take a look.'

Molly remained still and Olivia shrunk back into her corner, eventually Callie heaved herself up and Molly watched as she guided the officer towards the bedroom. She could hear the murmur of further conversation but couldn't make out the words. Turning to her friend, Molly saw the worried look on her face. 'Are you worried about her Liv?'

'I am, but also, I'm dreading that the police are going to call our parents. I really can't cope with that Molls. They won't take it well.'

Olivia's eyes filled with tears, and she seemed to close in on herself. Molly knew Olivia struggled with her parents, well, her mum and stepdad. It sounded like she could do nothing right. Unless her stepdad had been drinking. Then he would be very affectionate. Too affectionate. No wonder Olivia stayed at all her friends' houses as much as possible. Olivia didn't really talk about it. She never had, but she gave Molly enough hints for her to have a rough understanding. Molly shifted sideways on the couch, draping her friend in a hug. There wasn't much she could say to reassure her, the police probably would call their parents, but she wanted Olivia to know she'd be there for her.

'MOLLY' Callie was shouting from the upstairs landing.

Molly reluctantly got to her feet and Olivia followed. They traipsed up the stairs to find out what Callie was shouting about. 'Where is Ria's stuff?' Callie questioned before they were even in sight.

Molly stepped into the bedroom still stifling with the fumes from their body sprays. She lifted the bed cover, revealing the space under the bed where Ria had stored her bags. Confused, Molly took a breath and looked around the room, looking in every hidden space beneath beds before marching through the rest of the house. Ria's bags were missing, but in the kitchen, Molly found her diary. She'd never normally look in it, but now she felt drawn. She decided not to give it to the police unless something inside was relevant. She slipped it into a drawer to check out later. It was likely to be silly notes about friends and music and maybe the odd boy she liked, but nothing the police would need to know, and Molly knew Ria would be mortified to have strangers reading her private thoughts.

Molly watched as the others filed down the stairs, PC Davies was holding a packet of pills. 'I'm off now, I'll do some digging and be in touch later. In the meantime, call this number and quote this reference if there's any news. She's probably just headed home or staying with someone else. Try not to worry.'

Molly nodded and smiled, listening to the sound of Callie shutting the door behind him as he left.

Callie burst back into the room, and Molly jumped, more than she usually would. 'She took my toothbrush, why would she do that? Also, did you know Ria was taking pills? They were under her pillow. The copper said he thinks she might have been taking them to help with study. He also said it can lead to psychosis if she's not been careful. Do you think that could be it? Do you think she could be confused about reality and that's why she hasn't come back?'

Olivia's forehead crinkled and Molly watched as she tried to put her thoughts together. 'If they think that, will they still be looking for her properly? What if someone's taken her and the police are just blaming it on her losing the plot?'

Molly turned to her friends 'None of her stuff is here either though. Are we missing something? Surely, she wouldn't just leave? I just can't believe she'd do that.'

'She wouldn't' Olivia shook her head, emphasising her point. 'No chance.'

Molly watched on, her heart thundering and her brain a chaos of *what if's*. Molly had realised that Ria was last seen by Callie and Olivia around 11pm, not that long after they'd gone to the club. Molly knew she was smashed before they entered and had no grasp of timings once she arrived. She must have been there at least an hour though as she'd had a drink and danced before she began to feel unwell and sat down. What if Tom, the monster that had taken advantage of Molly, had also attacked Ria. She pondered this and decided he might have had time.

Molly had told nobody about her experiences overnight, and nobody asked. She now wondered whether she should at least tell the police but the thought of that horrified her. She just knew they'd be full of judgement, and it wouldn't change anything. It wouldn't change anything for her, but what about Ria? She decided to wait and see. It might be that Ria had gone wild and would turn up later with a story of a crazy evening. Molly doubted it but she clung to the idea, both for Ria's sake and her own.

17 – Ria – 11/06/1996

Ria stretched her neck, her mind muddled and struggling to break through the fug and wake up. She felt heavy, like she'd been laid in the same position for a long time and had sunk deep into the mattress, encased by clouds. She thought about her bedroom at home and the wonderful familiarity, but something felt wrong, maybe even smelt wrong. She struggled to open her eyes. The lids felt weighted down like after a heavy night of drinking. She hadn't drunk much though, had she? As her consciousness returned more sharply, she remembered she was on holiday and not at home after all. Something still felt off. The unnatural light glaring down made her squint, her eyes still half closed and struggling to focus. As she became more aware again of her body, she felt the roughness of the fabric on her skin, scratchy and unfamiliar.

As her eyes grew used to the light, she blinked several times, wondering if she was in fact awake or still deep in a strange dream. She sat up, head swimming along with her vision. A small window showed the moon, glowing high in the sky. She could see there were brackets on the window, locking it shut. Deep inside, her stomach was churning. She tried with all her strength to be the calm and logical person she usually was. The bright yellow light from the ceiling strip light hurt her eyes and she used her hand to shield them so she could look around. The bed was a flimsy fold-out camping bed and she had been covered by a scratchy woollen blanket which she pushed to the floor. She noticed she was still wearing her clothes from yesterday and felt the clenching of her heart. Where the hell was she? Her skin tingled and her mind began to race. She tried to think her way out of the situation, surely there must be a sensible reason for being there.

She raised herself up on unsteady legs and crossed

the few feet to steps that led upwards. They were grey concrete, like the floor. The walls were all bare brick, and it was devoid of furniture, other than what she'd slept on. She stepped up slowly, cautiously, to the door at the top. She reached a shaky hand out and grasped the handle tightly. She turned and pushed and pulled the door, initially in a firm and controlled way but slowly becoming more frenzied until she was hammering on the door and kicking at it with the bottom of her sandaled feet. Tears streamed down her face as she screamed and shouted and pleaded until her throat was raw. Feeling the claws of hysteria taking over, Ria sunk down, sitting on the top step, her back to the door. Her heart hammered in her ears to the exclusion of all else. She tried to suck in deep calming breaths so she could think.

She sat, trying to regain her composure so that she could make a plan and get the hell out of the dungeon. She didn't know how she'd got here, but she certainly knew it didn't indicate a happy ending. Ria paused when she heard the softest of noises, breathing and quiet movements, the rustle of clothing. Whoever put her here was outside the door, presumably listening to her cries for help. Nausea rose up in Ria's throat and she raced down the stairs. Spying the bucket, she emptied her stomach, while swiping at the beads of sweat turning cold on her forehead. She would not give him, whoever he was, the satisfaction of screaming and crying again.

As she stilled herself, she had a flash of memory. A chance meeting on the way home, and then.... And then nothing. It was a blank. She had an idea now of who had taken her. Why and where were things she would have to find out.

First things first, what could she use here? The bare red-brick walls had no adornments. She set to work looking under the bed, hoping to extract springs but when she looked underneath, the fabric was held up with tension around the main bars. No springs. She folded the bed up and lifted it. It was fairly light but cumbersome. She doubted she'd be able to hit anyone with it without them seeing it coming and having time to stop it. She also doubted it would do enough damage to allow her to escape. The ceiling was surprisingly high for what she assumed was a basement. There wasn't anything else in the room except a bucket with a puddle of vomit at the bottom, and a bottle of water.

She was desperately thirsty but reluctant to drink something left by him. He might be trying to drug her. Again. She couldn't remember being drugged, but that was the point, she couldn't remember anything about getting here. She plonked herself on the floor and noticed her sandals. There were no heels on them, but they did have a small metal spike where the buckle was. She pondered whether she could hit him with her sandal or poke him with the spike but either option seemed fairly puny and easy to overcome. She traced her fingers over the rough surface of the bare brick wall. Something about the scratchiness on her hands helped focus her mind.

She sat trying to think about escaping and potential things to say to this psycho when he appeared. She was desperately trying to keep her brain busy enough that it didn't allow another thought to come to the front. A thought she knew was lurking but that she refused to acknowledge. Would she make it out alive? She'd heard the stories after all, of people going missing, only to turn up a week later in rural woodlands or buried under a patio. The thought of a body under something solid made Ria swivel onto her side, surveying the floor. It was flat and apparently undisturbed, other than a small indentation at the bottom of the stairs. Ria wondered if someone had been pushed down them at some point. As the thought pressed forward, she began to sing quietly, the act of remembering lyrics keeping her thoughts in a safe space.

She didn't listen to R.E.M often but something about the fast pace of 'The end of the world as we know it' was perfect to keep her mind focused. Not to mention how appropriate it felt.

Ria waited. It had been hours since she'd woken up and nobody had been back. The light outside had grown during the day and was now dimming again as the sun had moved to the other side of the house and evening approached. She'd been here since late last night. Ria had figured it was around midnight that she'd been taken. She had used the folded camp bed to stand on, but she could still only get fingertips to the high window. The brackets locking the window shut were immoveable. She considered punching at the glass, smashing it. At least then she'd have a weapon of sorts, but she could also injure herself in the process. She tried a few weak blows but couldn't get the strength to smash the glass with her arms fully stretched and only her fingertips grazing the glass.

She had unfolded the camp-bed after a few hours, needing more comfort than the concrete would allow. She was determined not to fall asleep though. She lay back on the bed, the darkness growing outside. Despite the yellow glow within the room, the ceiling was otherwise clear. *No cameras*, she thought. At least that was something. Perhaps she could pretend to sleep and attack him unawares when he came in. She only had to knock him over, give herself enough time to bolt up the stairs. As she thought this, visions jumped to the front of her mind. Her dashing up the stairs and a faceless man reaching out, grabbing an ankle, dragging her back down into this basement. A shiver shot through her.

She would not fall asleep, she would not fall asleep. CLICK. Ria bolted upright in pitch darkness. She must have nodded off. Eyes wide and staring around, trying to see in the near darkness. She felt relieved that the moon was large and gave a slight glow to the room as her eyes became acclimatised. The light that had glowed in the centre of the room all day was now out, and she felt more vulnerable than ever. Something about being able to see what was coming was reassuring and the darkness took away even that small comfort.

Bringing her knees up to her chest, she hugged them close, rocking gently and humming to herself, 'Here comes the Sun' by the Beatles. She'd first hear that song on a mix tape Molly had made for her and now loved it. It was a link to her friends, and to safety. It was calming and helped when she was trying so hard to stay in control of her emotions; every beat of the tune tethered her to rationality. She'd been gone all night; her friends would have alerted the police and they would take it seriously. Her friends would explain that she was not likely to have just stayed out without contacting them. The police will be coming. They will. Anytime now. She told herself this on a loop. She finally stopped when she began wondering whether they would be able to find her, even she had no idea where she was. Despite having the window, it was too high for her to see more than just sky.

There had been no further noise after the loud click and eventually Ria relaxed a little, presuming it was the sound of the light being turned off rather than anything more sinister. She didn't know why she was here and being left without contact was unnerving her. She couldn't see it in the dark, but she knew where the bottle of water was and kept licking her cracked lips, desperate for some hydration but still hesitant to accept anything provided by her captor. Knowing too, that she wouldn't be able to refuse indefinitely.

Drifting back into her thoughts she imagined what her parents would be doing now. Maybe watching the Bill or Sharp. They'd be enjoying their time alone before she returned in a few days' time. What would they think when they found out? Would they blame her, thinking she'd been misbehaving and got herself into this trouble. Would they know already? She supposed they probably would. Surely the police would contact them early in their enquiries?

She spent a long time thinking about her parents in their living room at home. Picturing every familiar thing. The coaster she'd given her dad for Christmas. Her mum hated it because it didn't match but her dad kept using it anyway. The sofa that was so well worn but still comfortable and comforting. The chair with the wooden arms where her dad always sat. The rug with its strange pattern that Ria used to trace with her fingers. As she thought this, she reached out her hand and traced her finger around the edges of the bricks.

Ria had tried to conquer her mind and stay calm, and she'd done well so far. She knew now though, that she would need to drink the water. She hauled herself off the bed and took the bottle. The room was still dark but now her eyes were used to it, she could see enough to move around. She held the bottle in front of her and used her fingers to trace around the lid. It still appeared sealed. She squeezed the bottle, no leaks that might suggest he'd made a small perforation. The choice was no choice at all. She could not live without water; she could not fight or escape without water. She snapped open the lid and glugged down half in one series of greedy gulps. Half was enough. If it had no effect, she would finish the rest later.

18 - Callie – 12/06/1996

The day after reporting Ria as missing, Callie woke feeling bleak. She'd been so frivolous with Ria's feeling throughout the holiday. If she was honest, throughout their friendship too.

Ria's parents were expected that day. The police had called them yesterday and Callie had called them too. She was hoping Molly would do it, but she'd refused and there was no way Olivia would do it. Callie had swallowed her awkwardness and called them. Mrs Roe answered after one ring calling Ria's name down the phone. Callie had done her best to apologise and fill in any blanks left by the police but before long, Mrs Roe was shouting down the phone at her. *It's all your fault, you're such a bad influence.* Eventually Mr Roe had taken the phone. A calmer tone advised her that they would travel down the following morning.

Callie had spent all morning waiting and worrying, further wearing out the old carpet in their holiday cottage. She had sent Olivia down into town earlier to get some photographs processed that they could use for a missing poster. She was expecting her back soon. In between pacing, Callie had written out the wording for a missing poster, in her perfect handwriting. She planned to get photocopies in the afternoon and then hand them out through the town. In a crisis, Callie always needed to be doing. Not sitting and waiting like she'd been forced to do all morning.

Callie now sat alone and exhausted in the living room. Molly had been alone in the bedroom for some time now and Callie hadn't even really given her a thought. It was only when Molly entered the room, pale faced and with a nervous energy that sprung from her eyes and every limb of her body.

'I was going to wait for Olivia, but I don't want Ria's

parents to show up before we can talk.' Molly spoke and sat down, a sadness seemed to be pulling at her limbs, a resistance she fought against.

'I read her diary' Molly continued.

Callie had sat next to her and was shocked. She knew Ria had a diary but presumed it was in her bag, wherever that was. 'Tell me what it says.' Callie looked Molly in the eye, hoping to encourage her to tell all and quickly.

Molly sighed and began. 'Lots of normal stuff. You being a bully, me being a witch. It also says that she had a secret boyfriend. When we thought she was going home early all week, she hasn't been. She's been meeting him. I flicked back to when we planned the holiday and she's been manoeuvring us since then. Her and this guy, Marc have planned the whole thing. We didn't even know he existed. Maybe she did just run away with him.'

Callie watched the tears stream down Molly's face. Callie found it easy enough to see the worst in people, but Molly was the absolute opposite. Callie knew that the thought of her friend betraying her, ditching her, would cut deep for Molly.

'Why didn't she just tell us?' Molly whispered, her face wet and eyes swollen. 'Are we so horrible she couldn't trust us with that?'

'I think I've been a bit of a bitch to Ria. She gets under my skin with her over-thinking and major fun avoidance. I didn't mean to drive her to this though.' Callie looked down. Threads of shame had been spreading through her body since they'd realised Ria was missing. Callie knew she could be prickly, particularly with Ria, but she thought it was all between friends. It was just their dynamic, wasn't it?

'Callie, you know the other day, we were doing that witchy spell thing on the beach. You don't think it was what we did do you? Some weird magical reaction? I know it sounds crazy but...'

A laugh spewed out of Callie, which opened the floodgates and tears started to fall from her too. 'We're not actually witches Molly. It was a bit of silly fun, nothing more.' Callie wiped her face, annoyed for allowing that side of herself out. 'Your book is old and quirky, but it's not real.'

Eventually, Callie jumped at a loud and urgent knock on the door that rang through the whole cottage. Molly jumped to her feet and Callie let her lead the way. They knew Mr and Mrs Roe hated them, so they'd been dreading this meeting.

Callie dreaded what they would say now, their daughter missing and news of booze and weed and random guys. She was curious too though, *did Ria's parents know about the pen pal?*

Eventually, Callie jumped up too and stood in the hallway behind Molly as she opened the door. Ria's parents stood on the step. Despite the circumstances they were as neatly turned out as ever. 'Has she turned up yet?' Her Dad's voice softer than Callie had ever heard it before. Callie saw Molly shake her head, while Callie's gaze trailed onto the floor, she was generally better at avoiding situations that made her uncomfortable.

Callie and Molly stepped back in unison, a silent invitation to enter. Mrs Roe's down-turned mouth made clear her feelings about the premises.

'We need to go to the police station but thought we'd look in here first.'

'Come and sit down, can I get you a tea or something?' Callie watched as Molly did the act she always did for parents. It didn't really wash with the Roe's but they nodded accepting the tea so that was something.

Molly left the room and Callie perched awkwardly on the window seat while the Roe's sat together on the sofa. 'I'm sorry. I really don't know what's happened. Have the police told you anything more?' Callie asked, trying to sound friendly but fearing she came off more needy and wheedling.

'Nothing that you're not already aware of I think. We haven't heard from them today. I tried to call before we left but nobody answered the phone.' Mr Roe smiled at Callie who tried for a small smile in return.

'We said we'd be there at midday, so we'll have a quick drink and then head over. Before we do, is there anything you girls haven't told the police. I know we seem strict to you, but we won't be angry, I promise. If there's anything, please just tell us.' Mrs Roe sounded softer than usual, and it hit home for Callie. Ria was her daughter; she might be a grumpy old woman, but she still loved Ria and would do anything for her. Like any mother.

'Well, actually. We were going to call the police today. We found Ria's diary. It wasn't with her bag, she'd left it in the kitchen. Anyway, we've read some of it and it seems that Ria has being seeing a guy all week called Marc. We didn't know and we need to tell the police. The thing is though, I think they think she's run off because her bag was missing, but I just don't believe it.'

'Where's the diary? Get it, quick.' Mrs Roe pounced on the new information.

Callie felt the awkward knots of betrayal in her gut. She knew Ria would be devastated for her mum to read her diary, but it was too serious now to hold back. As Callie handed Ria's diary to her mother, her hand shook.

Mrs Roe clutched the diary close to her for a moment, before opening it up and flicking through the pages. After a few minutes of scanning the words written by her missing daughter, Mrs Roe jumped to her feet. 'Come on, we need to give this to the police now.'

Callie watched as she practically dragged him from the room, shoving past Molly who was carrying four mugs of tea. 'Let us know if there's any updates' Callie shouted to their retreating backs as they scurried down the garden path and the door slammed, cutting off further attempts at communication.

***

Olivia returned to the cottage shortly after the Roe's had left. Once Callie had selected a photograph from those that Olivia had collected, she taped it onto the missing poster she'd written. The three girls then walked down the hill to the town centre. Callie could feel Ria's absence, almost like a physical pain and knew the others would be feeling it too, but none of them spoke about it, it was too raw.

First stop was a shop they'd seen with a large photocopier where they walked out fifteen minutes later with one hundred posters.

It was midday and the sun was burning hot. The breakfast café by the beach was bustling and the girls ordered bacon rolls to go. With hot rolls clutched in their hands they walked through the seating area, asking at each table whether they'd seen Ria, holding her picture up for them to see.

The response was generally head shakes and brush offs. In the far corner, a bunch of lads they had bumped into several times were nursing breakfasts they were too hungover to make much of a dent in.

'Hey guys, do you remember our friend, Ria? Have you seen her in the last couple of days?'

'Was she the boring one? No, not seen her, probably wouldn't remember if I did.' Snarked, a skinny lad who looked about nineteen. Clearly, he'd got nowhere with Ria this week then.

They continued down to the High Street, taping posters up on lampposts as they went. Outside the bank they saw the usual gaggle of yellow vested charity workers strewn across the area. Callie moved faster, thinking of the people they must see each day. She strode straight up to one of them. They'd spoken to him before, he'd even taken a photo with them. Before Callie could speak, Olivia had jumped in. 'Our friend is missing, have you seen her?' Callie said this while thrusting a poster under his nose.

The man smiled and Callie realised how attractive he was. 'It's Jasper actually and yes, I remember you. I'm not sure who your friend is though. Her face is familiar I think, but I couldn't place where from. Has she been missing long?' Jasper spoke sincerely and Callie, realising he knew nothing, was now ready to move on.

'We reported her yesterday, but she was last seen late the night before. Call police if you hear anything.' Unusually, Olivia grabbed Callie's hand and dragged her away. Callie was relieved, there was no point wasting time on a dead end.

19 – Jasper – 12/06/1996

Jasper had spent the morning in town, working. He didn't want to change anything about his routine. He wanted to maintain his visibility and friendly persona in the public eye throughout this transition period. That was the problem last time, he thought. He got so engrossed in the object of his attentions, that all else fell away. When Abigail turned on him in Weymouth, Jasper was torn. He loved her but the problem-solving part of his brain wanted to kill. It was the cleanest way to end things. That part of his brain wanted all loose ends tied up in a neat bow, and certainly not an ex-something with too much information about him running free in the world. His hesitation had allowed her to escape. He was glad now that he'd started using a different name each time he arrived somewhere new. If Abigail did tell anyone, she would only tell of Jonathan Proud. Jasper was sure that he looked very different now from when he was in Weymouth. He thought it unlikely that anyone would manage to recognise him. As soon as he'd had some time with Ria, he hoped they'd be able to move on before long. A new town, a new life.

Jasper made a particular point of speaking to Ria's friends when they walked through town with posters. 'Who's that?' he asked as the bossy one waved a poster under his nose. She looked less sure of herself than usual.

The fourth one, Olivia, answered. It seemed unusual to Jasper that she would take the lead in answering, she seemed mostly to follow the others.

'Our friend Ria is missing. Have you seen her?' Olivia looked at him, he could see the hope shining in her eyes.

Jasper fixed a gentle and sympathetic smile on his face and added an empathetic head tilt to reinforce the impression. He responded that he hadn't seen her, his mind churning behind his sparkling eyes.

The three friends drifted away, dragged by an unusually pushy Olivia, and Jasper watched. They'd handed him a poster, and he looked down at it now, crumpled in his hand with Ria smiling up at him. He tucked it behind the other papers on his clipboard and thought longingly of going home to his love. Hoping she would be ready for him on his return. Ready to be moved and join him in the house, properly. Not locked in the cellar; that was just a temporary solution that would need to be resolved when he got home.

Jasper stayed in town for a couple of hours. He was unconcerned by how many 'sign-ups' he made for his job, but he wanted to speak to as many people as possible and be seen and remembered. He wanted to make it impossible to contemplate him as a suspect.

***

When Jasper got home, he paused before slotting the key into the lock. He couldn't hear anything which was good, but his heart sank a little. He missed watching. It was great that she was now here and all his, but he missed watching her. He loved her expressions, when she was unaware anyone could see.

Jasper stepped away from the porch, now decided on his new direction. He crept quietly round to the rear of the house. Lowering himself onto hands and knees, he continued further until he was flat on his belly. He turned his head sideways and peered through the narrow window into the dim room below and allowed his eyes to adjust.

Ria was asleep on the bed, mouth hanging open, arms flung wide. She looked vulnerable and perfect. Jasper's eyes scanned and found the now empty water bottle and he smiled. It would make his job much easier.

When Jasper crept back to the porch and into the house, his stride was broader and his body looser. She had done what he needed her to do and that pleased him.

He listened briefly at the cellar door and was quickly satisfied on hearing a repeated muffled snore.

He opened the door and stepped down into the room where his captive lay defenceless. The smell was already pungent with urine and vomit, and he scrunched his nose in displeasure. He was determined not to linger. He stepped closer and looked at her deathly pale face. He reached out and pinched her cheeks. He knew it would bring colour to her but also wanted to ensure she was truly asleep and not faking it. He enjoyed the twist of her skin. The reddening blossoming as he released it. He bent closer then, stroking her face. He leant in and kissed her tenderly on her lips, slowly, lovingly, before biting her bottom lip, drawing blood that he licked away, a mixture of emotions bubbling within him, threatening to explode.

He mentally shook himself and stood up. She would not wake up for hours, but he had work to do.

He reached into his pocket and withdrew some cable ties and snapped them around Ria's ankles. He then tightened another around her wrists, tightening them just enough to nip at the flesh.

Once satisfied, he hauled her into a classic fireman's lift and trudged up the stairs leading to the main house. He had to dip his knees here and there to avoid scraping her on the low ceiling of the stairs.

Once he was stood in the hallway, he paused a moment, his breathing heavy. Once he'd recovered, he headed up the broader stairs of the house to the first floor. The floorboards creaked and Jasper's muscles heaved. When he reached the bedroom he had prepared for her, he lowered her gently onto the bed, stroking her hair back off her face. He took a Stanley knife from his pocket and loosened Ria's hands. He'd tied them while he carried her, just in case. Once free, he used a rope that was tied to each bed post to tie her arms outstretched. He was satisfied that she wouldn't have much freedom of movement.

Jasper draped a hand along Ria's legs. Her skirt was hitched up slightly from when he placed her on the bed. Joy bounced in his stomach at the delicate, pale skin and the knowledge that it was now all his to enjoy.

Jasper looked at Ria's face, still slack mouthed. She was dead to the world, he thought. Then he laughed inwardly at the irony of the thought before reminding himself that it wouldn't come to that this time. Ria certainly wouldn't behave like Joanne. He hadn't wanted to hurt Joanne, but she'd attacked him. That was the first time though and he'd learnt a lot since then.

Jasper now had other matters to deal with. Before leaving Ria, he cut the tie around her ankles, he did not think she would be able to escape the rope, and the ankle ties might just be too cruel. When he cut them loose, Jasper caressed the raw red bands etched into Ria's skin, his mind flashing to similar marks he had inflicted before. A maelstrom of emotions surged through his body. He wanted to protect her, and if someone else hurt her, he would destroy them. He couldn't deny though, he enjoyed watching the marks blossom on her skin. Delicate eruptions of pleasure echoed deep within him. Bright, dazzling but just a little painful. When Abigail had escaped him, she had been covered in tokens of his love in shades from purple to yellow and everything in between. She shouldn't have escaped.

Jasper knew he had things to do, but he took his time, watching and touching and enjoying her placidness in sleep. He knew when she woke, she would be angry. He hoped she'd get over it quickly though, as he knew he would struggle to maintain restraint if she pushed too hard. He hoped his other guest would encourage Ria to behave, once he told her about him anyway. Jasper had taken him before he'd taken Ria. He would be weaker now, hungry and thirsty. Jasper had given him a small drink and snack, but he was more than happy if he suffered a bit. He certainly didn't want him feeling strong.

Jasper stood, his hand tracing over Ria's face before he left. He really ought to check on his other guest.

20 – Olivia – 12/06/1996

Olivia chewed her nails, or at least what was left of them. She had been out with Molly and Callie most of the day, showing posters to everyone they could and speaking to people. She felt like there was so little that she could do. She wanted to hammer on doors and drag people to the police station. It was unlike her to feel so fierce, but she still worried the police thought Ria had just left and run off with her secret boyfriend. Olivia had watched Molly try to explain and later, when the police officer had popped by to update them, she'd stressed the point too. She still didn't think they really believed it though. She knew that meant that minimal resources would be used to find her. Olivia felt powerless, as she often did and wondered at what point in her life she'd feel like she was holding the reins herself.

She was alone in the living room of the holiday cottage. Molly was sleeping upstairs, and Callie had stomped out of the house twenty minutes previously, seemingly unable to settle and covering her worry with rage as she often did.

A heavy knock rang through the empty space and Olivia jumped. She raised herself up and stepped into the hallway to answer the door. The police officer in charge of Ria's case was there, in a tired looking suit that seemed to hang off him in remembrance of a time when his frame had been more substantial. The formality was enough for Olivia to feel intimidated. She offered a small smile and opened the door wide for him to enter.

'Where are your friends?' he asked, sitting down on the sofa.

Olivia thought he was trying to be friendly which made him a little more approachable. 'Molly's sleeping and Callie's out. Is there any news?' As she finished speaking, Olivia raised her eyes to meet the detective's, pushing against her usual shyness.

'We haven't found Ria. We have had another report of a missing person though. Her boyfriend, Marc. Marc's friend also insists he would have told her if he was running off with Ria. She also said he hasn't even taken his wallet. We have decided to link the cases and upgrade them to High risk. This allows us to allocate more resources and gives us more power to investigate. I know that none of you knew about Marc. Now you've had a chance to think, is there anything else that we should know about? Any details about Ria's behaviour, anything she said? Anybody you've met this week that has worried you or bothered you?'

Olivia sat quietly when he spoke but inhaled deeply when he mentioned the case being upgraded. She hoped now it would be taken seriously. 'I think Ria took my toothbrush instead of her own. I really can't think of anything else. There was Nathan who was a bit pushy, but we told you about him already. I mean we spoke to loads of people, but nobody stands out. Ria didn't really have much to do with anyone we got chatting to. She would chat, but she wouldn't get too close to anyone. We didn't have any arguments with anyone either.' Olivia was speaking and desperately trying to think of some useful nugget of information that would help, but she came up blank. She really didn't have any idea of where Ria was. She only knew it wasn't by choice.

After further rehashing of the same information, where the detective seemed to be testing information, he eventually rose to his feet and Olivia stood too, uncertain of how to behave.

'Thanks for stopping by Detective.....' Olivia hesitated, she couldn't remember his surname. She felt the heat rise in her face.

'Detective Inspector Phil Campbell. Phil is fine.' He smiled and Olivia felt reassured again, wishing she wasn't so affected by other people.

After he'd stepped out, she closed the door, leaning back against it and wondering what she would hear next time the police came to the door. She was still stood like that, back against the door when Molly drifted down the stairs yawning. 'Was that the door?' Molly asked, halfway through a yawn.

Olivia now followed Molly through to the kitchen. Olivia reached for the kettle, happy to have something to busy herself with. 'It was the police, Detective Inspector Phil Campbell. They've upgraded it to High risk so maybe they'll find her now. He said Marc had been reported as missing too and didn't even have his wallet. I think that was enough for them to realise they hadn't planned this. He kept going over everyone we've met this week. I couldn't think of anything we hadn't already told him.' Olivia bustled around making tea while giving her friend the update. Olivia did notice Molly looking worried, biting her lip. She could also see her twisting her fingers together and fidgeting. She wondered if there was maybe something that Molly hadn't shared. 'I've left his card on the table if you think of anything else.' Olivia said this and watched as Molly hitched on a smile and responded. 'No, we've told them everything'.

Olivia didn't like confrontation, so she didn't push further, but she did make a mental note to watch her friend a little more closely. She was definitely hiding something.

Olivia noticed that for the rest of the day, Molly had a thoughtful expression, intermittently shaking her head. It looked like she was facing an internal battle of some kind. Olivia had racked her brains to think of what Molly would be worried about, but she had no idea. She thought that it surely couldn't be too serious?

***

Olivia's phone buzzed in her pocket. Dave. Her thumb hesitated over the button before she finally accepted the call. 'Hi' she said in a quiet voice that reflected how small he made her feel.

'Liv, what's all this? We got a call from the police. What have you girls been up to?'

'Ria's missing. We didn't do anything. She'd only had a couple of drinks, she didn't do anything wrong.' Olivia felt herself jumping to the defensive, but she couldn't help it. Every word he uttered felt like an accusation.

'Your mum's working, but I'll come down tomorrow. I'll stay with you girls, keep an eye on you while we figure out what's going on.' Dave sounded almost pleased at this plan. No doubt it ticked some boxes for him but none of them were about keeping Olivia or her friends safe.

'There's nowhere to stay, Ria's parents are here. We're fine, honestly. We'll be back in a couple of days, I'm sure they'll find Ria soon. Honestly, we're fine.' Olivia could feel the sting of tears in her eyes, threatening to take over, the shake in her voice was already obvious. There was space in the house, but she didn't intend to tell Dave that.

'Well, I'll talk to your mum, and I'll let you know in the morning. Alright, behave yourself and maybe see you tomorrow.' With that, Dave hung-up the phone and Olivia's body shook violently as tears flowed freely. The knot in her stomach felt like it had been viciously twisted. Now she wouldn't even know if he was going to turn up or not. She knew she'd have an even more sleepless night ahead.

Olivia plonked herself on the sofa, swiping away tears with her sleeve. She could feel the heat rising to her face. She hated him. Even at this time, with Ria missing, he was just thinking about perving on her and her friends. He certainly wouldn't help anything. All Olivia wanted to do was think about her missing friend and do everything she could - sadly not much - to help. The last thing she needed was to be worrying about Dave turning up with his wandering hands. She would not subject her friends to that. Molly had an idea of what he was like and would hopefully guard anyone from being alone with him, but Olivia had never been open with Callie. She dreaded that she'd make a joke that she just wouldn't be able to cope with. Olivia now felt weighed down, not just with the displeasure of Dave potentially attending, but because she would no longer be able to keep her home life to herself. It was something she'd never shared outside of her house. Even Molly had only guessed bits and pieces and was good enough not to make her talk about it. Maybe she would phone her mum later and get her to stop him coming.

Callie walked into the room, interrupting Olivia's churning thoughts. Olivia smiled and offered her tea. If in doubt, tea was always an easy distraction.

21 – Molly – 13/06/1996

Molly stood on the corner of the road, trying to build up the courage to cross and go into the police station. The road was busy with what she presumed was mostly tourists, both driving and on foot. The heat of the day had added to the sweat pooling in the small of Mollie's back. She'd normally have a spliff to relax but decided that was not a good idea before speaking to police officers. She lit up a regular cigarette and inhaled deeply, enjoying the rush to her head. She decided to wait until she'd finished the cigarette before approaching the pollce station

She watched as Nathan North stomped out of the back door of the police station. It was still early, and Molly wondered if he'd been in a cell overnight. He looked baggy eyed, like he hadn't slept a wink. He was wearing what Molly guessed to be a police issue grey tracksuit and plimsols

As he strode nearer, he walked straight into Molly. She had tried to move out of the way but found her legs unable to move, her feet planted on the floor.

'Sorry, er…" he said, seemingly confused but also with Molly thought, was a flash of anger in his eyes.

'It's Molly, we met earlier this week.'

'I know who you are' he grunted, trying to get past her, each of them ducking sideways, making it impossible for either to move forward. Molly could smell the stale sweat from Nathan, his hair too attested to his lack of shower that day. Eventually they both stilled, and Nathan stepped sideways and began to walk away.

'Were you talking to the police?' Molly called as he began to walk away.

He stopped and turned, looking at her. 'I didn't do anything to your mate. I've told the police everything I can and now I just want to be left alone.'

'Why did they have you in there, if you didn't do

anything?' Molly asked, suspicious of his attempts to get away.

'I was there because of how I was with Ria. I don't even like her. I only did it to keep my mates off my back' Molly watched Nathan scrunching his face. Suspicious of his saying he didn't like Ria. It's not how it looked the other night.

'Why though? Why are your mates on your back Nathan?'

'I'm bloody gay alright! I'm not out and I don't want you telling anyone. I was full on with Ria because I thought my mate was getting suspicious. I'm sorry alright.'

Molly watched Nathan's eye welling up and with that he turned and walked away, without a backward glance.

Molly watched him walk away, now satisfied that Nathan was not involved. It made it even more important for Molly to do what she'd gone there to do. She slowly walked across the road and rounded the corner to the front of the police station.

She stood outside the large glass doors, forcing down gulps of air. Her toes kicked at the cigarette butts and old coffee cups strewn around the entrance, evidence of many worried waits and caffeine pre-loads before confinement.

Through the glass she could see the small reception area. An old woman sat, bouncing her knees nervously and looking at the internal door at every sound. Molly could see the man behind the desk; he was in uniform, and she swallowed down the nerves that kept bubbling up from her tummy. Molly had a final pull at her own cigarette and stubbed it out with her battered flip-flops.

It was time. Molly raised her hand and placed it flat on the solid metal panel of the door, the cold as she touched it calmed her slightly, and then she pushed and stepped through. As the door swung closed behind her, it blocked out the noises from the street and the quiet enveloped her. Each footstep towards the counter felt intolerably loud, the seated woman's eyes trained on her every move.

Molly reached the counter, and the officer kept his eyes down on his newspaper. 'erm... hello?' Molly hesitated, eventually drawing his gaze.

'Hello Miss. What can I do for you?'

'Is there somewhere I can speak to you, privately?' Molly looked down, at five foot eight she was fairly tall but in that moment, she felt like she was folding in on herself and shrinking. She crossed her arms tightly around herself.

'Would you rather talk to a woman?'

'Yeah, probably, can I?'

'Hang on'

The officer turned and walked away, leaving Molly leaning against the counter. It was several minutes before an internal door to Molly's left opened and the face of a woman poked through, signalling with her eyebrows and a nod that Molly should follow her. She led her into an interview room away from eavesdroppers and sat down, arm outstretched indicating Molly should sit down too. The woman wasn't in uniform and had a lanyard hanging from her neck. 'I'm DC Payne' she said while holding her identification up for Molly. 'What have you got to tell me?'

'I'm Molly. My friend Ria is missing, and I think there's something I should tell you, but I don't want my friends or anyone to know.'

Molly sat, hands twisting together on the table in front of her, highlighting her gnawed nails. She looked up through her curtains of hair.

'The thing is' she began, 'I don't really remember that much. I know nobody will believe me and I would just deal it with myself but if there's a chance it's connected with whatever is going on with Ria then I thought I should speak up.' Molly began twisting the ends of her hair, doing all she could not to be forced to make eye contact as she told her story.

'Why don't you tell me everything you can remember. Sometimes details that you think are not important can make all the difference.' DC Payne had a kind face and when she smiled at Molly, she felt more able to tell her story.

'I think that I might have been raped.'

***

Ninety minutes later, Molly ducked out of the police station, lighter in many ways but with eyes still flicking nervously, hoping not to be seen.

DC Payne had been kind and had made lots of notes while Molly was talking. She said she'd investigate and let her know whether it was linked to Ria's disappearance. She would also let her know if they found any evidence like CCTV that could help confirm whether anything had happened. Molly still felt like she didn't want to proceed with a prosecution, but she was glad she'd at least shared what she knew.

Molly had been offered to have tests done with a doctor to see if there was any forensic evidence still present. She declined. It had been three days, and Molly had showered more than she had in her life. The thought of a doctor poking around down there also horrified her.

She left it, with a sigh of relief, in the hands of DC Payne.

22 – Ria – 13/06/1996

Ria felt the tickle of her hair on her nose each time she breathed. Her eyes fluttered and darted around the old-fashioned room. Her ears detected very little, perhaps the gentle mooing of a cow in the distance, and birds chirruping on and off. The faint smell of cooking lingered in the air and Ria's stomach rumbled an involuntary response. She instinctively pulled her arms towards her, ready to heave herself up, but she felt an immovable tug on both of her wrists. Slightly frayed blue rope was wrapped around each wrist several times, tightly secured to a bed post on each side. She was forced to remain on her back, but her legs were untethered. Ria forced herself to lay back a moment and breathe deeply, trying to swallow down the panic that was rising with heat through her body. Slowly she tilted her head, first left, then right but neither knot seemed particularly yielding. She shuffled her bottom backwards, so her head was supported and the strain on her wrists eased slightly. Scanning the room she saw an old dark wood wardrobe, with a key in the lock of the door. On top, a couple of boxes, presumably holding hats from weddings through the years. A small basin with a mirror above sat in the corner by the window, the basin chipped and the tap dripping. The window was hung with thick nets and heavy, overly-patterned curtains hung either side. The curtains were faded from years in the same position, in the sun that was currently streaming onto them. There was little else. Nothing to inform her of where she was or who had placed her here. The wooden door was closed and so far, she'd not heard a peep from beyond it. As the thought of silence entered her mind, the fear penetrated it, engulfing her. She'd been focused on the practicalities of getting free, looking for anything she might be able to reach. It was only after noting the silence she began to wonder why she was there, how it had happened and who was responsible.

She'd woken before in a basement and now she wondered how she'd ended up in a bedroom. The thought of these huge blackouts in her memory made her shudder. She remembered drinking the bottle of water and now realised it was exactly what she'd suspected. Laced with God knows what and designed to place her at his mercy. Again.

Ria tried to move various parts of her body, systematically from toes up to her head. She realised that she ached all over in a dull but tolerable way. Her right knee however, seemed particularly sore and stiff. She had no idea how long she had been there, but the need to go to the toilet was beginning to rise.

Until now she had been relatively silent, unsure and afraid, building tension through every nerve in her body until the point when a noise she'd never made in her life, exploded from her lips. She screamed and screamed until her voice was breaking and tears streamed down her face. The pressure built in her lower abdomen and eventually, with no other option, she released and felt the warmth seep around her and dampen the sheets beneath her body. Shame burned her cheeks, stoking the fear that had taken root in her gut.

***

Ria woke to the sound of the door handle being turned, she shivered both from fear and from the dampness she was wrapped in. Her eyes wide, she watched as the door crept open and a man stepped into the room. He was tall and attractive with floppy hair, and he smiled affectionately at her. For a moment, she almost forgot everything under his warm gaze.

She remembered bumping into him on the way home. It was him and that mesmerising gaze, before she felt a scratch on her arm as she bent down to pick up her necklace.

Ria froze, her lip quivering as anticipation rose. He stood there for what felt like an hour, just staring at her. Up and down. The smile on his face fading as his eyes roamed, before finally closing them and drawing in a deep breath. He opened his eyes, now with a coldness that seemed impossible moments before and turned and marched from the room, closing the door firmly behind him.

Ria yanked at the restraints on her arms, and hysteria built in her chest, threatening to explode, as she tried desperately not to allow it to take over again.

While she struggled to maintain control of herself, the door opened once again. The man stepped in, knife in hand and strode across the room, around the foot of the bed. The shrieking noise she emitted was alien to Ria, she had no control and was lost in terror. Her neck strained as she jutted it towards him, screaming, pleading and whimpering. He paid no attention, merely scowling as he moved, a look of disgust showing in the downward turn of his mouth. He sliced quickly and efficiently at the rope on Ria's left hand. She pulled her hand in towards her chest, quickly and scooted backwards to the far bed post, where her right hand was still trapped and began fidgeting with the rope to no avail. The man moved quickly around the bed and stood again in the doorway. 'Strip the bed then take off your clothes'.

His voice was hard and cold and invited no objection. Ria's mind raced with thoughts of being wrapped in these sheets once he'd killed her and him disposing of DNA. She thought these things, but she also stripped the bed. He was still holding a knife, and she had no idea what his plan was. She must try to keep him placated until she understood better.

Once the bed was stripped and piled at her feet, Ria hesitated. Jasper did not speak, merely motioned with the knife towards her clothes. Tears streamed once again down Ria's cheeks, but she didn't make a sound this time. She quietly removed her clothing, piece by piece until she was standing naked and vulnerable in front of this monster, who leant in to free her arm of a strap but slicing through it with his knife. 'There's a box under the bed. Fresh sheets'.

He said this in the same cold voice and left the room. He returned a few moments later with a bin bag and a summer dress, her summer dress that she'd brought on holiday. He threw the dress at Ria who gladly pulled it over herself between pulling sheets over the corners. She could not reach the bottom corners and could not insert her right arm in her dress. 'Put the dirty things into the bin bag'.

Again, Ria felt she was disposing of the evidence of herself having been here, but she complied, there was little choice. Once she filled the bag and placed it back on the floor, the man took it from the room. When he returned, his smile was back. 'I'm going to cut this rope off so you can finish the bed and put the dress on correctly. Be warned, I will not hesitate to punish you if you try anything'.

He brandished his knife while speaking, but the smile was back, it was bewildering for Ria to try to understand his motives.

Jasper cut the rope, and Ria did as she was asked. For some reason, his eyes on her while she put her arm through the shoulder strap of her dress felt almost more invasive than when she was naked. Perhaps it was because his pleasure was now obvious, his smile wide. Ria dutifully neatened the bed and then stood, looking for further direction. 'Sit down'.

The dark pools of his eyes would have been hypnotic in other circumstances. She perched on the edge of the bed and then shuffled further back when he motioned her to. He then sat beside her. Close. Too close. His hands were in his lap, as were hers but when he turned to talk to her, she could feel his breath on her and felt violated by his proximity. He still held the knife, balanced on his knee, the point aimed at her. 'I'm Jasper, do you remember me?' Ria nodded

'Now, tell me everything about yourself. Everything'.

Ria paused and Jasper's smile began to fall. She began to speak. She told him she was on holiday with her friends and just carried on spewing words, eventually changing subjects when she needed to carry on. Providing she was talking, Jasper seemed happy. She dared not allow his smile to fade again.

Ria enjoyed chatting but this endless prattle about herself was not an easy task. Eventually she was saved by the bell as an alarm blared from the neighbouring room. 'To be continued,' he said, rising to his feet.

Jasper stood and pointed towards the head of the bed, signalling Ria to move there. She did and he slowly re-tied a rope, first around her right wrist and then her left. He stood and surveyed his prisoner and then turned and left without another word, closing the door behind him.

Ria remained still and silent, listening to the sounds of her captor moving through the house. First the alarm was silenced then the slow stomp down the stairs, and eventually the firm closing of the front door. Shortly after which, a car engine started outside and slowly faded, and she presumed the car was driven away.

Ria breathed deep, relieved to be alone but wondering how Jasper had her clothing. If he took her clothes, would her friends think she had just left?

23 - Neil/Jasper – 04/04/1979

Neil sunk into his bed, doing his best to stay out of his aunt's way. He made himself comfortable, resting his head on his entwined arms and allowing his mind to wander as his eyes fixed on the blank ceiling. He was getting no answers from anyone else about where his dad was, he thought he might figure it out if he looked back on his memories. Maybe there would be a clue somewhere that he'd missed.

He didn't really know what he was trying to remember, so he let his mind drift to whichever memories forced their way to the front. His dad's face was the first thing. Grizzled and stubbly. The creases, a testament to the expressions that accompanied his wild changes in temperament. Laughter lines, yes, but also the ones that erupted on his forehead when he scowled and raged.

As he thought of his father's rage, Neil remembered a moment at nighttime. He'd crept out if bed, desperate for the toilet but on the way, he'd heard some strange noises he couldn't place. Whimpering and a rhythmic thudding. He tiptoed closer to his father's bedroom door from where the noise sprung. The door was slightly ajar, and Neil could see the source of the thudding noise. His father was pacing back and forth, fast and fiercely in his heavy boots. His hand clutched something long and flexible that dragged on the floor as he moved.

As Neil watched he saw behind his father, the bed and the shape of his latest mum laying on it. Red lines criss-crossing her body and tears streaking black makeup from her eyes, down her pale face. Her hands were tied to the top of the bed. Rope bound round and round. The look of devastation on her face struck Neil. He stood watching, unsure what to do. Shaking at the thought of his father turning round but not wanting to leave her tied up like that. In his hesitation, he froze. Neil now realised what his father was carrying, a belt. He watched dumbstruck as his father cracked it across the middle of the woman, she groaned but clamped her lips together, seemingly trying not to make much noise.

'I warned you' Neil hated it when his father's voice growled like that. Even he knew it meant danger.

Neil felt anger bubbling in the pit of his tummy. *Why didn't she just behave?* He thought. If she just didn't make him angry it would be ok. They might be able to watch tv and eat ice-cream and Neil knew his dad would laugh again. He was so much fun until they did something wrong.

Neil snuck away to the toilet. He didn't flush the chain, just crept back to bed. He didn't want his father to turn on him. In bed, he squeezed his eyes shut and pulled the duvet in tight around his ears.

24 -DI Phil Campbell – 13/06/1996

Detective Inspector Phil Campbell had been rummaging through reports all morning. The clear suspect in this case was the boyfriend, *it often is* he thought but something about it just felt wrong. There was always the possibility that they'd run away together, but everything about the girl suggested she wouldn't do something like that. The family and friends were all shocked to learn that she'd planned this holiday to secretly meet Marc, and that she had been secretly meeting him all week. Maybe nobody knew Ria Roe as well as they thought they did.

It was something they may never know unless they managed to find the girl herself, presuming they did that while she was still alive of course.

Phil Campbell thought of his daughter, she'd just turned sixteen. Younger than Ria but close enough to know how it would feel if she went missing or was taken. If the family say she would never leave like this voluntarily, he had to believe them.

Phil flipped open a notepad and began to map out connections, creating an unwieldy spider on the page. *Surely we've missed something* he thought, determined that if he looked hard enough, something would jump out at him. There had been an article in the local news, suggesting the girls were promiscuous and had essentially asked for this to happen. It made Phil rage, they could get as drunk as they wanted, they didn't deserve this. Small town mentality was something he had always struggled with. Even in the station, he'd heard the officers talk when they thought there was nobody listening. Everything seemed to be the victim's fault. Everything. Phil knew, no matter how drunk or out of control he became, he would never hurt someone in the ways he had seen happen while doing his job.

Looking at the phone reports, Phil could see that Ria

and Marc had planned this rendezvous months back. The accommodation had been booked by phone by one of the other girls, Molly, in February, but it had been Ria that had been determined about the dates, now it was clear why. It was new to have personal call logs, only a couple of years ago, a lot of this communication would have been through phone calls on a landline rather than text messages, but having the exact messages in black and white made it easier to figure things out.

Marc and Ria had made the plan together, but Marc had suggested the date and also the location. Ria had then agreed. Could Marc have orchestrated something here. Marc mentioned in one message that he would be traveling with a friend, but he doesn't give a name. Looking further down the data to 10th June, Phil could see that there was no activity beyond 8:04pm when Marc text Ria asking *hope to see you tomorrow!* Ria had replied with a selection of kisses, and then nothing else after and both phones appear to have been switched off since. Although Ria connected to a phone mast showing her phone was on around 11pm. The fact that his phone went off grid before hers made Phil wonder, was that because he was planning something?

Phil traced through the other numbers that Marc had contacted. They'd mostly been bottomed out by the team, and he could see no loose ends there.

Next, Phil leafed through a stack of statements; nothing jumped out to him. He was often last in the office. He liked the quiet to go over the day's progress, sadly today there was less than he'd hoped for.

Making some last notes to kick start the following day, Phil closed his notebook and neatened his desk. Sometimes, he just needed to walk away to see the bigger picture. A good sleep would settle the pieces in his mind, and he hoped then he'd see the way forward. His shoulders, rounded from years hunched over a desk, ached and he rotated them, trying to loosen the knots. Grabbing his coat, he walked defeatedly from the office, flicking the lights off as he went.

Walking out of the front doors of the police station he waved half-heartedly at Sandra, who'd drawn the short straw of staffing the station reception for the night shift, and left the station. The night was dark, and the rowdy nightlife could be heard drifting through the air. Phil walked slowly, allowing his attention to catch fully on anything he saw, blocking out the case that had been rattling around his mind for the last few days. Down the hill, he passed the Town Hall with its tatty noticeboard outside, with locals asking for house sitters and gardeners and all sorts of other tasks. The mundanity of it made him smile and feel more like himself again. He continued home and by the time he'd opened the front door, felt able to leave his work outside before greeting his wife and peeking in to see his sleeping children.

25 - Ria – 14-15/06/1996

Ria heard her captor in the house in the night and early in the morning, but he hadn't come to the room where she was trapped. She felt exhausted from lack of food and drink. Surely he didn't bring her here to starve her to death? The last thing she'd heard was the thud of the front door. It caused her a sense of relief that he was out of the house but the fear too that he wouldn't come back and she would die where she lay, unable to free herself.

The sounds of the car engine and crunching of gravel faded, and Ria knew she had to try to free herself again. The knots this time had been tied more hastily, and she hoped that meant she had a chance. She pulled and rolled and wriggled her left wrist until it finally gave a little. After that, she was able to unravel the rope from her wrist, and it was free. The adrenaline drove through her body, she felt like she could do anything. One knot, that was all, and she could do it. As she began to feel the rush of joy and the taste of freedom, her stomach dropped, hearing the rumble of an engine stop outside. She tried to be fast and silent, but the other knot was tighter, no wonder Jasper had needed a knife to free her. Tears burst from her eyes as she realised, she wasn't going to be able to undo it in time and tried to lace her left hand back into the rope to hide her attempted escape.

When the door to her room opened, Jasper's eyes took in the scene immediately and his face dropped into a stony expression once more. 'I'm sorry, I was uncomfortable. I wasn't trying to escape I just needed to move a little'.

Jasper nodded at her, silently. His silence drove fear into her, perhaps more than shouting would have, it felt unnatural. It wasn't just the silence, his face changed, the light left his eyes and his features seemed harder somehow. Jasper turned and walked out of the room but returned shortly afterwards with a sandwich and a bottle of water and placed them down where Ria, now with one hand free, could reach them. She felt clumsy trying to eat with her left hand but was relieved that he hadn't instantly tied it up again. She drank the water greedily, afraid of needing the toilet or being drugged but desperately thirsty and not knowing when she would get more.

'I want us to be happy Ria, but you mustn't try to leave. Now put your left hand here, on the floor.'

He pointed and Ria hesitated, unsure what to do, and afraid of what would follow. She edged across the bed and off, onto the floor. Still tethered by her right wrist, she reached her left hand low, fingers trailing the floor. She thought perhaps he was testing how far she could reach. 'Flat'.

He barked this, impatience raising the volume and sharpness of his voice. Ria lowered her hand flat feeling the grain of the wooden floorboard cold beneath her palm. Jasper inhaled deeply before stomping fiercely on her hand with his booted foot. Ria cried out, drawing her throbbing hand towards her. Unsure if her fingers were broken or bruised. Without pausing for a beat, Jasper rounded the bed and pulled her left arm away from where she'd held it to her chest. 'Please, it hurts. I won't do it again. I'm sorry', Ria screeched through snot and tears, but her words fell flat. The shock seemed to freeze her, leaving her unable to do anything but cry. She should have expected violence, but he hadn't been violent so far and she'd begun to think she might be able to talk her way out of her situation.

Her arm was wrenched and tied tightly, far tighter than before. The throbbing was enough to make Ria dizzy, in fact, she realised she felt like her consciousness was ebbing away. Jasper stood over her, his figure becoming a shadowy mass before her head fell forward and she was gone, temporarily spared the pain that would follow.

***

When Ria's fuzzy head finally allowed her to open her eyes again, she was relieved that she was alone. It was mere moments before the pain in her hand throbbed and she winced. She looked as closely as she could. Her hand was swollen, her middle finger particularly was at an unnatural angle. As she thought to herself, *don't move*, some reflex misunderstood and she twitched her middle finger, causing a shooting pain down through her wrist. Her hand was red and swollen and she struggled to look at it without retching.

Ria's eyes moved on, she looked down at the rest of her body and shook her head, blinking away her confusion. She was wearing different clothes to when she had nodded off, but they were her clothes. She wondered how he had more of her clothes. Her toes had been painted, and she noticed a floral smell of perfume about her too. Her stomach reeled at the thought of him touching her while she was unconscious.

Ria began thrashing about in panic and disgust before she accidentally pulled at her left hand, causing such a sharp splice of pain, she stilled her limbs to breathe through it.

I need to play along Ria thought to herself. *This sicko wants to feel like we're together or friends or something. I'll need to make him believe it until there's a chance to get away.* There was nothing she could do then but wait. Her wrists were tied too tight for her to release them, and she didn't dare be caught halfway again, she shivered to think what he would do next.

When Jasper eventually re-entered the room, Ria sat up and gave him her biggest smile. 'I'm sorry about before, I'll behave now, I promise.'

Jasper smiled and seemed happy, she just needed to keep him that way. 'That was a taste for you. I don't want to hurt you, Ria. If you disobey me again, I will punish someone else on your behalf. I have the Frenchman, and he will be hurt, more than you've been hurt, if you try to ruin this.'

Ria's mind reeled. Marc, that meant he also had Marc. Fear clenched her heart in a vice but outwardly she remained composed and looked down, guarding her expression.

***

Dawn broke and by Ria's reckoning, she'd been missing for two days. It was hard to tell as she'd been drugged and was in and out of sleep constantly. She might have slept for twenty-four hours, but she didn't think so.

Jasper was asleep on the bed next to her, naked, like her. A thin sheet draped across her belly, but her breasts, left exposed, made her feel vulnerable.

He hadn't touched her sexually, at least not when she was awake. Each time she woke however, it was clear that he had touched her. She was unsure of how far he'd gone or what he'd done. She could smell soap and perfume, it was almost like he'd cleaned her, the thought of which sent shivers through her whole body. He had painted her nails a ghastly red which somehow horrified her as much as the cleaning. The thought that he'd pored over her while she was unconscious, churned the miserly contents of the stomach. She struggled with the uncertainty of the situation. The not knowing was hard to cope with and she kept running scenarios through her mind of what he might have done. After playing too many horrifying scenarios in her mind, she realised that thinking about it now would not help her. She tried to push it down, deep in her mind. She hoped at some point she'd escape, and she would deal with the unknown then.

She had decided that she needed to make friends with her captor. She'd read an article on it once and the girl got away by befriending her abductor. He seemed to be desperate for their imaginary 'relationship' to be real. She hoped if she could play along, he would eventually let his guard down. If he at least released her hands, she was sure she'd find a way out.

Ria tried to turn her mind to something happier, something to keep her going. Not Marc, now that she knew he too was trapped, any thoughts of him caused her blood to pump and a screaming rage to descend. She could not do that now. She thought of her friends. The strange group that had formed years ago and somehow managed to ride the storms they all faced through school. Ria knew her relationship with Callie was difficult, but she'd give anything to see her now. To hear a snidey one-liner or be called a square. Would Molly or Olivia have noticed she was missing before Callie? Probably, she decided. She wondered how they were feeling. How soon would they call the police or her parents? How would they possibly find her if they did?

Ria reflected on the details she knew about her abductor. She knew he worked in the town centre, signing people up for donations to the animal shelter. It took her a while to remember that. She also knew his first name was Jasper, but even that could be fake. She could think of nothing that would make the police connect her and Jasper. Nothing, that if they investigated, would lead them here. The only option was to find a way to escape; she couldn't afford to rely on being rescued, she would need to rescue herself.

26 – Jasper – 14/06/1996

Why? Why did she have to try to free herself? Jasper paced fiercely in the living room. Ria had forced him to hurt her. He hadn't wanted to, but she'd really left him no choice. He hoped that now Ria knew he had the Frenchman, she would behave. He could see just how wonderful things could be if she would only do as she was told.

Jasper placed every ounce of blame on Ria and blustered about as if stomping on her hand hadn't given him a sense of pleasure. He was aroused and all he now wanted was to lay with her, but he knew he needed to calm down first. He couldn't allow himself to lose control. Not yet anyway.

Jasper used his energy to replace all the boxes in the basement. He'd removed them, leaving it empty for Ria, but now he'd settled her upstairs, he was happy he could restore the basement to its former use as a storeroom.

It took around half an hour for Jasper to move everything, by which time, he felt calmer and more in control of himself again. Closing the door in the basement, he raised his eyes, looking up the staircase. He was ready.

Walking with measured steps up the stairs, Jasper opened the door to the bedroom, just enough to look in. He could see Ria's head, still hung down. Her body limp and vulnerable. She'd passed out from the pain in her hand and the sedation in the food had kept her unconscious.

He moved about the rooms, gathering what he needed. After she'd urinated on the bed, the room hadn't smelt the same. She needed a wash, and he needed the intimacy of her touch. He knew it would take some time for her to get close to him when she was awake, but he needed something to keep him going. It was only fair. He was helping her really, nobody wanted to fester in their own stink. He would help her.

Jasper set about washing her with a bowl of soapy water. Tenderly cleaning every inch of her body, expressing his love through his care of her. He removed her clothes to clean her, leaving her naked beneath a sheet. Enjoying the peace he had found with her, he stripped off his own clothes and lay next to her, watching her. Her skin was so pale, like a flawless china doll. Jasper rolled off the bed and collected a knife from his trouser pocket and cut a lock of Ria's hair, curling it around his fingers, the medium brown showing flecks of different colours as the light hit it from different angles. Jasper took the lock from the room, placing it on the pillow of the room he had been using.

When Jasper re-entered the room where Ria lay, still unconscious, he sat himself at the foot of the bed and gently massaged Ria's feet, before painting her nails in bright red nail polish. Next, he took a hairbrush he'd placed on the bedside table and gently brushed Ria's hair. He smoothed it down over her shoulders, before pulling his hands back. He didn't want to get carried away, he wanted her to love him and see how he looked after her. There would be time later for more.

Stepping from the room, Jasper decided to go through everything in Ria's bag. He'd taken everything he thought was hers on the night he'd taken her. Mostly the bag was full of clothes but stuffed in an inside pocket was a stack of letters. Jasper slowly unfolded the first of them. There were no envelopes, but each letter was folded individually. He fancied he could smell traces of ink and Ria's perfume as he unfolded the paper.

Dear Ria, he read, *I'm glad we spoke on the phone, it was so nice to hear your voice. I think we should do it. My friend went to St Afan in Cornwall a couple of years ago. Perhaps we could go there and meet up properly.* And so it continued, encouraging Ria to meet him and convince her friends to go along with the plan.

Jasper opened another letter. *Ria, one week to go. I can't wait to see you, and if I'm honest, to kiss you too. I feel like the last couple of years have been leading towards us meeting. I don't know if you can be in love before you meet someone, but I think I am.*

Jasper could feel the blood pumping through his veins, threatening to explode. He eyed a small fireplace, central to the room where he usually slept. Scrunching up the opened letters he threw them into the grate. Drawing a lighter from his pocket, he flicked it to life and began to burn the other letters, one by one, dropping them into the grate as the heat of the flame began to nip at his fingers. Once all traces of his rival's loving words were destroyed, Jasper breathed deep, expelling the tension and heading back to the neighbouring room.

He curled up on the bed next to Ria and watched again. The gentle intake of breath and then the exhale, her body utterly relaxed and all his. The pure innocence of every part of her mesmerised him and he soon drifted off to sleep, contented.

The streets that had looked bright with laughter and temptation a few days ago now looked bleak to Callie. Every face a threat, the memory of laughter turning to hysteria in her mind.

Callie had built her character on being tough, not caring and pushing boundaries. Now she felt devoid of purpose. Why did she always have to play games with people? To jibe at them until they reacted. The snipey jokes she always made at Ria's expense were playing like a slideshow in her head, taking her through the various hurt expressions she'd put on her friend's face. Friend. She'd called her a friend while simultaneously mocking, pushing and deriding her. What kind of a friend was she. Clearly a bad one.

Callie had left the cottage early. Olivia and Molly were still making toast and sipping tea. They asked her to wait, and she'd said she'd see them in town. She just couldn't bear to sit around any longer.

As she walked the streets of town, eyes wide, she saw shifty faces, veiled in secrets. She could see Ria's face smiling back at her from some of the posters she'd stuck up on bus stops, trees, railings and anywhere she could on previous days. On one lamppost, someone had stuck another poster over the top. Callie tore at it, shredding it and watching the slivers of paper drift down the street in the gentle breeze. How could someone cover a missing girl with a karaoke at the local pub?

She felt like she'd already been to the local shops and cafés and felt overwhelmed by the need to do something, anything. She really had no idea what else to do.

She decided to approach the people, milling around the High Street, perhaps some of them hadn't yet seen the posters or heard about Ria's abduction. She purposely said abduction to herself because, despite initial doubts by the police, she knew Ria wouldn't just run off with a man she barely knew. That was something she was sure of now she'd had the chance to think about it.

'Hi, have you seen my friend, Ria Roe, she's been missing for four days now.' She spoke while waving a poster in front of a middle-aged woman's face.

She did at least pause, really looking at the poster before shaking her head. 'Sorry, I've never seen her before. I hope you find her,'

She spoke kindly but had begun to walk away while she was still talking. A cloud seemed to fall around Callie as she realised people really didn't care. Unless it affected them, they just wanted to walk away and ignore the suffering of anyone not connected to them.

She sat on a bench in the High Street, wondering what else she could be doing. She put the posters down on the bench beside her, placing her bag on top to stop them blowing away. She drifted into more reminiscences of how awful she had been and suddenly became aware that someone else had sat on the bench.

'Do you think they are together?' Callie turned at the smooth French accent as the young woman now sitting on the bench spoke to her.

'What?' Callie's patience was almost non-existent, and she had no interest in random chit-chat.

'Your friend, do you think she is with my friend, Marc?'

It was only then that Callie really looked at her. She saw her perfectly styled hair, delicately painted nails and a sense of style that seemed alien to Callie. The woman's forehead was crinkled in concern and Callie wondered how close her and Marc were. She hated herself for thinking it, but she'd pick her over Ria any day.

'Sorry, what's your name? And what do you know, tell me everything.' Callie stared intently at this woman, she needed to get answers.

'I'm Clementine Dubois. I came on holiday with my

friend Marc Girard. He wanted to meet a girl, your friend Ria, and I agreed to come along. I haven't seen him since Monday 10th June and I think it is the same for you with Ria? Marc wouldn't just leave me here. No way.'

'And the police haven't told you anything else? You haven't heard anything more? They've told us next to nothing and it's driving me crazy.'

'That's all I know. Here, this is my number. If you hear anything, let me know. If they're together, Marc will look after your friend.'

'I hope so', said Callie as she watched Clementine stand and walk away. She looked more like a model than a teenager and despite everything else going on, a flame of jealousy ignited within her. She really wished she could be a nice person, like Molly or Olivia. Or even Ria. Why didn't it come naturally to her.

Callie sat on the bench, drained of all motivation and lacking any direction. Eventually, Olivia and Molly flopped down on the bench beside her. 'Nobody cares', Callie said, without even looking at them.

'We're supposed to be going home tomorrow. What do you think we should do?' Molly spoke softly but Callie could hear the conflict of emotions as she spoke.

'Maybe we could go speak to the lady. I think my Mum will give us the money for it if I ask. We can't leave here without her. I couldn't go back and live normally without knowing she's alright.'

'I'm broke but if your mum will pay for the cottage, I'll stay. I don't want to leave her either. I feel like there's something we've missed and if we can just remember then we'll be able to figure things out. I can't think of anything though.' Callie desperately wanted to pluck a useful nugget of information from her brain.

'What about you Liv?' Callie looked at her friend, quietly nibbling at her nails.'

'I'll stay if you are.' Olivia gave a small smile then

seemed to drift back into some kind of daydream that Callie had dragged her from. Callie stood, leading the way back up the hill.

'Come on then. Let's ask, then we can decide.'

Marc had initially been the prime suspect for DI Campbell, but as the days passed, he had to admit, it seemed less likely. Everything about his background checked out. Within a day of being contacted, his parents had arrived and were helping fully with all enquiries. After speaking to Mr and Mrs Roe, they also doubted his involvement or any suggestion that Ria might have just run away.

DI Campbell's team had been scouring CCTV of Ria's every move in the small town since her arrival. A young officer called Matt Gardner had recently broken his ankle while detaining a serial rapist that had been wanted for many months. The public thought of him as something of a local hero. Whenever it was mentioned, PC Gardner glowed red, feeling it was more a case of being in the right place at the right time.

DI Campbell knew that Matt Gardner was likely to be off the streets for months, a real blow for an active young officer. He had allowed him to latch onto this missing person case. He felt that the more resources they could throw at the case, the better. PC Gardner had come to him, asking to trawl the remaining CCTV footage and he gladly agreed. It allowed him to keep everyone who could be, out looking for the missing girl.

***

When DI Campbell went to see PC Gardner in a neighbouring office for an update, he was pleased to see he'd gone beyond the basics. He'd set up a board full of faces. Post-it notes were strewn across them describing when and where they'd been seen and who else was present. In some cases, one photograph was surrounded by a selection of others.

To DI Campbell it was indecipherable, but he was confident that PC Gardner had a system.

The desk to the side of PC Gardner was strewn with takeaway boxes and wrappers from chocolate and sweets, testament to how long PC Gardner had spent in that room poring over CCTV in the last couple of days. The Detective inspector winced at the old food smells that lingered in the room.

'Gov', Matt nodded at the senior officer as he entered. 'I've got three that seem to crop up more than the others. It might be nothing, but they're at least leads to follow up'.

'Right, sounds better than what we've got next door. Talk me through it'.

Matt took a file he'd prepared, he turned to a large and empty desk in the corner and used his crutches to hobble across. He emptied the images onto the table and shuffled them into the right order. There were at least three images for each person of interest. On the back of each image, a time, date and location recorded along with Post-it notes containing any additional information. The board was his working out area, and this selection seemed to be his conclusions.

'The first guy I think looks like the chap they met in the pub, Nathan. He's been around a lot, notably at times when Ria seems to be away from her friends. Not much else on him. Then, I've got these two. This one wears a fluorescent vest and often has a clipboard, I think he works for the local animal shelter, but the image is too pixelated for me to be sure. At one point, this guy seems to attack Nathan, just after Nathan and Ria have spoken. The other guy has been with Ria a few times. I haven't seen a picture of the French guy yet so I guess it could be him?'

'Wow, thanks Matt, yeah that's Nathan and that's Marc so now that leaves me very curious about this guy. Can you put together as much footage as possible with this unknown man. Also, look out for any sightings with any vehicles. And see if you can pin down who he's working for. Well done lad, I'll see if any of the other local bobbies know him. Shout if you find anything else.'

With that, the detective inspector took an image of each man and left to brief his team.

As he returned to his own, open-plan office Phil Campbell wasted no time. 'Charlie, speak to the council, find out which charity has been canvassing the High Street and then find out who has been out on their behalf. Tom, get Nathan back in, grill him again and find out whether he had a run in with a charity worker in the town centre. Matt has CCTV if you want to watch it first. Lara, get the latest on Marc, if he's been found, I want him in, if not, grill the girlfriend again. Cross-question them, talk to each other. If they've done nothing, they may at least have seen something. Charlie, I want a name for the mystery man by the end of the day'.

A roaring chorus of 'yes boss' followed by a flurry of activity as Charlie, Tom and Lara, the detective sergeants under DI Campbell's command each disseminated these and other jobs to their teams.

29 – Ria – 15/06/1996

Bile rose in Ria's throat, but she fought it down. She could not afford to give into her feelings, she had to do what needed to be done, to get out.

She had woken up naked again. Jaspers pale form motionless beside her. Ria's hands were still tied. She shifted so she was mostly on her side, her body curled in towards Jasper's. Her left arm pulled painfully on the rope, but she pushed that pain down deep inside. Timidly she moved her feet, so they were entwined with his and gently relaxed her head on the pillow beside Jasper's. She wanted him to wake and think she'd been watching him lovingly. She needed to build the picture he wanted to see.

When Jasper's eyes fluttered awake, Ria smiled in her most innocent and attentive way. With no mirror to practice in, it was guesswork. Her insides fought against such shows of affection, and she feared her true feelings would be visible. She could feel her nostrils attempt to flare and thought that must be her 'tell'; the thing that shows she's lying.

'Morning' Ria whispered to Jasper as if she too was newly awoken from sleep. Jasper paused before responding and Ria hoped she'd not misjudged her tone. 'Good morning', he eventually said while stroking Ria's hair and planting a kiss on her forehead. Ria relaxed a little. It was strange how he could be almost tender despite the fact that he was holding her here against her will. Did he really believe they could have a future? His face told Ria that he did. She didn't know if that was terrifying or reassuring. If he wanted a future that meant he didn't plan to kill her, and Ria certainly found that comforting.

'Jasper, do you think at some point I might be able to have a shower? I want to look nice for you, and I feel dirty and horrible. I won't try anything, I just want to be clean'. Ria looked up at him, trying to evoke innocence.

'Hhmm, maybe later, I'll see what I can do. I only want to make you happy Ria. You and me forever. I would do anything for you. As long as you don't try to leave'.

Ria smiled back contentedly and meekly said a 'thank you' while looking up through lowered lids. She again pushed down the sickly feeling rising from her stomach and maintained a placid expression. It would be hard to maintain but she knew now it was the only way out.

***

When the door creaked open later, Ria looked up, arranging her face into a welcoming smile. Jasper looked at her before speaking. She thought he was somehow analysing her before coming to a decision. 'I'm going to let you have a shower. I need you to know though, if you try to escape, you won't. You won't escape and your friend Marc will be punished instead of you. I hope you understand that'.

Ria nodded in what she hoped was a deferential way. 'I promise, I just want to get cleaned up, that's all'.

With that Jasper opened the door wide. Ria could sec across the hallway another room that seemed to be lacking a door. It had chequered lino on the floor, and she presumed it was the destination for her shower. Jasper walked behind her and slowly sliced away the rope from her left wrist. Ria winced, her left hand was still swollen and bruised and as the rope was released it began to throb, presumably due to the freer blood flow. Ria felt nausea gurgling in her stomach with each pulse of pain. She hoped being drenched in the shower would help.

Jasper walked back around the bed and stood before Ria. He placed a cable tie around his own wrist and another, interlaced through it that tied around Ria's left wrist; homemade handcuffs. Jasper then cut through the bindings on Ria's right wrist and she slowly shimmied off the bed, using her right hand to push herself forward.

Jasper took her left hand in his own, they were cuffed closely together anyway. Pain shot up Ria's arm each time her middle finger was touched, and she felt tears falling down her cheeks. She didn't want Jasper to see tears and desperately tried to swat them away with her right hand. He led her across the landing and into a bathroom with an avocado suite that had seen better days. A trail of limescale was visible beneath a dripping bath tap. The frosted glass of the window distorted the view outside, but Ria could see a large building close by.

A chain of cable ties was attached to the bath tap and as Ria stepped in, Jasper tied her ankle to it. She couldn't move far, but enough to shower without toppling over. He then cut the tie on her wrist with the knife he always carried. 'I won't sit here and watch, I'm not a pervert, but I'll be just outside so don't try anything silly'.

Ria nodded and when Jasper stepped out of the room, she pulled the summer dress she was wearing over her head and dropped it on the floor before turning the dial for the shower. The initial burst was icy cold but felt so refreshing. She held her left hand in the cold, letting it numb the pain a little. As the heat grew, she stepped beneath the flow and allowed it to wash away some of the trauma, for a few moments at least. She closed her eyes and thought of her bathroom at home. Imagining stepping out onto the fluffy green bathmat and curling up in her soft and oversized dressing gown. When she eventually opened her eyes, she felt calm and began to look around the bathroom. There were a few broken tiles and old Rawlplugs poking out of the wall, where she presumed old shelves had once been fitted. Jasper had clearly removed everything that would normally be found. All she had was some shampoo, conditioner and a bar of soap. While washing, she turned, staring out through the distorted window. Other than what appeared to be a building, the landscape looked bright and full of green. She suspected they were out in the countryside, no longer in or near town. She continued to scrub and rinse and scrub again, never feeling quite clean enough. Once she was finally done, she turned off the water and rubbed herself dry with an old and well-worn towel that had been left on the sink. Once dry, she wrapped her hair in the towel and stepped into her dress again. She sat on the edge of the bath, unable to fully get out while one ankle was still tied. 'Jasper, I'm finished. Thank you', she called, hoping it was the right tone, the right words. It was hard trying to predict what a psychopath wanted to hear at any particular moment.

Jasper stepped back into the room, she could feel his eyes on her, scanning for changes. Finally, he used a cable tie on her wrist again, bonding her to him and then he cut her ankle free. Ria felt the relief, her leg muscles were beginning to cramp from being in the odd position. When she looked at Jasper, she couldn't help but think he had a slightly frenzied expression. Perhaps because she was showering, but he'd left the room so that didn't seem to fit. Once she was back in the bedroom the dread filled her again at being tied up.

'What about if you tied my hands together? It's so uncomfortable when they're pulled out. Please Jasper, I'll behave, I promise'.

Jasper looked at her; she felt that he was weighing up his options. 'Alright, sit down.'

Jasper closed the door behind them as he entered the room, he was blocking off the potential exit. She perched herself on the edge of the bed and Jasper began looping cable ties to the bed frame but allowing a little more space for movement. Ria's hands were tied in front of her and attached to the chain. 'Thank you'. Ria spoke simply. She really was grateful, despite the throbbing pain in her left hand. She'd begun to feel the flutterings of panic at the thought of her arms being spread apart again. Now, hands together she felt a little more in control of herself, less vulnerable.

When Jasper left, Ria made herself comfortable and began to think about where she was. She'd heard seagulls daily but that didn't necessarily mean she was right by the sea. She could smell the sea sometimes, and when she looked through the bathroom window, she saw green but then sparkling beyond that made her wonder if it was the sea beyond.

If she escaped, if she found a way to get out, what would be the best way to go? There was obviously a road at the front as she'd heard the car most days. That would be where he'd look for her though. If she headed towards the sea, could she follow the cliff line back to town? Might she have a better hope of escape that way? She also had to think about Marc. She now thought the building outside was a barn and that perhaps that was where Marc was. She hadn't heard any noise in the house to suggest he was nearby. Unless of course he was in the basement now that she'd vacated it. She'd have to check both.

The evening passed away quickly as Ria's mind whirred with thoughts of how to escape and how to get Marc away without him being hurt. She was sure that she had a better chance with her hands tied together. She wouldn't try anything tonight; she would behave and hopefully he would relax more. She would wait until the time was right.

30 – Olivia – 15/06/1996

She should have been heading home today, after having the time of her life. Olivia turned over in bed huffing, not yet ready to face the day. This was supposed to be the holiday of her young dreams where she found herself and embraced her freedom. Instead, she felt like a scared child. Scared of finding out what had happened to Ria and frightened too, of having to go home and face the music. Her stepdad would certainly enjoy telling her all the things she and her friends had done wrong.

In the last few days when Callie had been talking about whether to head home, Olivia had still had an over-riding feeling that Ria would just turn up and they'd head home as planned. With three hours left until their coach home would leave, Olivia knew now the absurdity of the hope she clung to. She felt a darkness envelop her and ducked her head under her duvet, removing the light that seemed to taunt her. Hope was a false promise, and she would cling to it no more.

Her phone clutched in her hand as it had been every waking moment since Ria had left, buzzed to life. *What time does your bus get in?*

She'd texted her mum already to say she would not be on the bus. Why could he not behave like a normal person. He was clearly already looking forward to her return. Quite in opposition to her own feelings.

Olivia jabbed at her phone with her finger. *I'm not coming back until Ria is found. I told you both already! If I had anywhere else to go, I wouldn't come home at all!*

She pressed send and shoved her phone under her pillow. She vaguely felt further vibrations but refused to look at the response he'd have sent.

Olivia peeked out from her duvet, spying Callie still out cold on her bed and looking up towards the top bunk, she could see Molly's hand draped over the edge. She crept out of the room, glad of the fresher air on the landing and crept down the stairs to the kitchen. The cold floor felt good after the clamminess of the bedroom. She splayed her toes, trying to find some sense of grounding herself, something she often did to feel calm. She stood waiting for the click of the kettle boiling before carrying a steaming cup of tea into the back garden. They hadn't been outside other than when they looked around on the first day. Now Olivia felt like she was seeing it without the rose-tinted glasses. There were three battered garden chairs, two of which had rungs missing from the back. The matching table was in the far corner, on its side with one leg missing. The small garden was boxed in with hedges on two sides and a fence with a gate at the back. It would be sufficient for her current needs.

Olivia pulled the only stable-looking chair into a patch of sunshine and sat, with her legs hugged in against her, and her heels resting on the edge of the seat. For a moment she just closed her eyes and enjoyed the feeling of heat on her skin. Since Ria had been taken, they'd spent every minute answering questions, putting up posters and speaking to anyone that would listen to try to find a clue that would help. This felt like the first time she'd been awake and able to be still and silent and alone. She often spent a lot of time with her friends, but this continued confinement together made Olivia realise just how important it was for her to have alone time. Her sanity depended on it. She still worried for her missing friend, but she needed to allow some peace to filter through her body, or she'd be good for nothing before long.

When she felt her core become just a little more composed, she finally opened her eyes. She squinted at the brightness and realised her sunglasses were still in the bedroom. She turned her face away from the sun and towards the house where her eye was caught by something on the top of one of the hedges. Something that seemed to be mostly orange. It was above Olivia's height, but she put her tea on the floor and dragged her chair over to the hedge. She stepped up, feeling the sway from the unstable chair, and reached out, grabbing a small, crocheted orange sofa. Ria loved the television show Friends and had lots of memorabilia. It was a key ring, and icy tendrils looped themselves around her heart. It was Ria's keyring that was usually hanging on the zip of her large travel bag. She wondered how on earth it could have come to be abandoned there. She hugged it close before realising it might be evidence and quickly jumping down and running into the kitchen where she placed it in a food bag.

It might be nothing, she thought, but she ought to tell the police. She stomped back up the stairs, her mind too abstracted to walk quietly. The bedroom door flew open under her touch and she grabbed her phone and she was heading back downstairs as she heard the grumbles form Molly and Callie at their rude awakening.

Olivia dialled the number for the detective inspector and took a deep breath. She hated having to speak to people she didn't know. It was worth it though, if it helped make sense of what happened to Ria.

31 – Jasper – 15/06/1996

He knew she was the right choice. Even now, so soon, she was already changing. He wasn't stupid though, he'd have to make sure she wasn't faking it. He didn't think so though. For all the time he'd been watching, she had always seemed straight up, no falseness at all.

When he'd woken up in the morning to her gazing at him, he'd felt like he was in heaven. He had paused before speaking, trying to swallow down the smile that was trying to burst forth. To feel her toes curling around his own, legs entwined, without having to ask her. She just did it. She must realise he just wants to love her and for her to let him. She certainly deserved a treat of some sort.

She'd asked for a shower and Jasper though, he could manage that without too much trouble. He also thought it would be a treat for him. After lunch, he put some loud metal music on in the upstairs landing. He hated it, lots if angry men shouting. It almost gave him a sore throat just listening to it. It was necessary though.

He removed the bathroom door. He didn't want to risk her locking herself in and climbing out the window. Not that he expected her to, not now.

Then he set to work on what he really needed before he could allow her to shower. He had tried first with a manual drill, hoping he could do it quietly, but he just couldn't get through the wall. Now, with a soundtrack for disguise, he aimed the electric drill and made a quick hole through from the landing into the bathroom. In the bathroom, he snipped a Rawlplug, tucking a small ring from it into the hole. It made it look like an old hook had once been there. His spyhole was hidden in plain sight.

Later, when he let Ria into the bathroom and secured her, he slipped out and took up his station. Her face looked different when she was alone. As if every muscle was finally able to be free and exactly itself. No unwilling smiles or false friendships. The tilt of her head backwards as she rinsed the bubbles away, drifting down her body and over her leg where the cable tie pulled at her, nipping her.

By the end, Jasper could feel himself drifting into their future life together, all problems washed down the drain with the shower water. He refused to dirty the experience by turning it into some sort of sexual perversion. He kept his trousers on and his hands on the wall, but he couldn't deny the excitement.

He watched as the shower was turned off and knew it was tlme to move on.

***

When Jasper finally shut the bedroom door, leaving Ria secure behind it, he headed downstairs to the kitchen. He'd given Ria a treat, now he thought he might give the other one something too. Rummaging in the cupboard, Jasper grabbed two crackers and placed them in a food bag. He added a lump of cheese from the fridge and re-filled a plastic bottle with water from the tap. That was plenty, he thought. He could afford a small treat to keep his guest going but certainly didn't want to spoil him.

He headed out of the back door, head tilted up, enjoying the heat of the sun on his face. He looked forward to a time when he and Ria could be outside together without him worrying that she'd try to run. His mind wandered over future adventures they could share from climbing mountains, to kayaking. The future began to unfold within his mind, and he almost forgot what he was on his way to do.

He hoofed the large plank barring the barn doors up and out of the way. He left it leaned on one of the brackets to make it easier to replace once done. Stepping into the cool cover of the barn, Jasper could smell the old, dusty smells of a place storing items that never get used or moved. Musty. That was probably the best word for it. He couldn't hear anything below and knelt a moment to listen before hauling the cover off the pit where he'd stored his other captive.

Mr Glamcoe, who owned the house, had said it was a pit for fixing cars. Jasper looked down as the shape of Marc unfurled and stood. Jasper realised it couldn't possibly have been used for cars, nobody would be able to reach them, it was too deep. That was a mystery for another day.

Jasper watched Marc stand, impressed at his movement despite several days of minimal food and drink. It worried Jasper and he nearly denied him the food he'd brought. It's her treat, not his, he thought and decided he wouldn't deny it. Marc was still tied to the ring on the floor and Jasper was pleased he'd not been able to loosen those ties.

Jasper stood, looking down and Marc had yet to say a word. He'd expected shouting and swearing and threats and begging, but Marc just looked up, eyes locked on him, silence the only power he had retained.

Jasper held the food bag and bottle of water out for a moment, before dropping them to Marc. Marc didn't miss a beat in catching them. A sign his reflexes were still sharp and should not be under-estimated.

Even when catching the offered food and drink, Jasper noticed Marc did not drop his gaze. It felt like a challenge and Jasper could feel the pulse booming in his head as the anger built. He stepped away without covering the pit and then grabbed a glass jar from a nearby shelf, throwing it with pace at the floor of the pit where it shattered into a mass of shards and splinters. His blood still burning from the defiance, he reached for the hose that hung on the wall. He turned it on and blasted the walls of the pit. He was careful not to aim directly at his prisoner. He wanted the dirt and glass to be scattered by the water and thrown up at him by the force of the water.

He slammed the wooden cover back over the hole, securing it down with some bricks. 'Good luck avoiding that in the dark'.

Jasper felt his mood had been impacted badly by Marc's defiance. Perhaps Ria would need to pay the price. It might be the only way to keep him in line.

It was his eyes that had angered Jasper, so perhaps something had to be done to hers. Nothing permanent of course; he loved her eyes, but enough to show Marc where his defiance would lead. It would wait until tomorrow, Jasper thought. Now, he would need to head back to town and be seen working as expected. Keeping up appearances was beginning to wear on him, he hoped it wouldn't be for too much longer.

Molly fidgeted with her hands, searching for the right words. 'We all care about Ria. I'm not saying we give up on her, just that maybe we should head back and do the last exam and then maybe come back after. We can't just give up on our futures. Do you think the exam board will just give us the grades we deserve if we don't turn up?'

Tears sprung from Molly's eyes as she spoke. Talk of leaving felt like a physical pain in her heart, but she didn't want to have to give up on university and her future. If staying in St Afan would help Ria, she wouldn't dream of leaving but she felt useless. She'd been trying to stay busy with posters and things, just like Callie and Olivia, but nothing had come from it. There had been a buzz the previous day when Olivia had found Ria's key ring on the top of the hedge, but the police took the information along with the key ring and they'd heard no more of it.

Molly finally made eye contact with Callie and recognised the hard edge in Callie's eyes and the tiny shake of her head that confirmed she would not be leaving. She looked at Olivia who seemed to fall apart in front of her, sinking down onto the sofa. 'I can't leave Molls, I just can't.' Molly thought Olivia's face was almost pleading with her to understand. Of course she did. Molly had already decided that either they all stayed, or they all left. She couldn't bear to leave another friend behind, even for a short time.

'Alright, we stay.' Molly sat next to Olivia. She knew she appreciated physical closeness when things were tough. 'I have to say it. I know nobody wants to but…. What if they never find her.'

Molly could feel the strength of Calie's anger from across the room. 'We're not going home without her. End of.'

When Callie spoke, it was dangerously quiet, and Molly

shrunk into herself as she watched her stomp from the room. Olivia pulled away from her and curled on her side on the sofa, shaking her head to also presumably say no.

Molly couldn't deny, she felt the same. The thought of never seeing Ria again still just seemed so unlikely, but she couldn't deny the rational side of her brain that knew they couldn't stay indefinitely.

Molly stood, grabbed her purse and walked away. Her mind drifted over the past week or so since they'd been in Cornwall. Every chance encounter.

Her mind was busy, but her feet led her forward. When she became aware of her surroundings again, she was standing in the centre of town. Many of the people were familiar; she'd seen them several times over the last week. This small town was beginning to feel like home.

Molly had no reason for heading out other than giving her friends some space. She spotted a small café a few doors away and headed in. There was one person queuing ahead of her, a businessman in a suit who seemed very out of place with everyone else in beachwear.

She hadn't noticed anyone else come in behind her, until his voice made her jump. 'Have they found your friend yet?'

Molly spun to match a face to the friendly voice. 'Oh hi, no we haven't. No news at all really.'

Molly gave her standard reply that she'd given to countless people that had asked when they realised, she was *one of the friends*.

Her mind refused to offer up a name for this man and eventually Molly asked 'Sorry, what was your name again? I know we've spoken but there've been so many people we've spoken to this week.'

'It's alright. Jasper' he said offering Molly his hand.

Molly placed her hand in his. He was warm and soft, and it felt nice to speak to someone friendly after the volatile conversation with her friends earlier. 'I'm Molly. You do charity sign-ups don't you? We did try and dodge you one day. We're all students so no money for that just yet. I will give regularly when I'm older though.'

Molly shook herself, what was she wittering about? Jasper didn't seem to mind. He smiled at her, and she relaxed a little. 'Next please' was shouted from behind Molly, she guessed by the staff behind the counter. She stepped forward and Jasper stepped forward with her.

'Could I please have a tea, to drink in.' Molly spoke to the waitress and then glanced around to ensure there was a table available.

'I'll get that, and I'll have a black coffee too. Thanks'

'Oh, thanks. You didn't need to. It was nice of you though. Thanks'.

Before long, Molly was sat at a small and slightly sticky table opposite Jasper. She wondered how that had happened, she hadn't really intended on sitting with him.

Jasper had incredibly piercing green eyes. They had tiny flecks of hazel and were mesmerising. 'Why don't you tell me about your friend? It might help to talk about her.'

Molly stared at Jasper, then realised he was right. They'd all been so careful, trying not to say the wrong thing. What she really needed was to talk. To think about Ria and all the good stuff, that was what was going to keep her going.

'Well, I suppose she's probably the sensible one out of all of us. She doesn't drink much and sometimes it's frustrating when she tries to make us slow down or something. She cares though. She always looks out for us, and she has great taste in music. Awful taste in men going by the celebrities she likes. She's clever, hoping to go to Oxford and I know she will. She will. It's funny because I think we all take her for granted a bit, not realising how much she brought to our group. We're all different and her kind of different is as good as mine or the others. Why did we always act like her difference was a bad thing?'

Molly paused for thought and Jasper maintained his gaze on her. She'd have felt uncomfortable if those eyes were not so addictive. 'It does feel better to talk about her, thanks.'

'Go on then, which celebrities does she like, give me a laugh.' Jasper winked at Molly, and she could feel the flutters of attraction coursing through her.

'Well, I'm not naming names, but if there's a group of people and there's one old and unappealing one, Ria will probably fancy him. I'm saying that but now we know she secretly had a boyfriend and has been meeting him all week. I'm wondering whether she was just throwing us off the track. Maybe that was her way of not getting involved in our silly games.'

Molly had slipped deeply into her own head again, thinking of Ria and whether she really was who Molly thought she was at all.

'It's been nice chatting Molly, but I've got to go. Ria will be fine. Trust me.'

As soon as he finished speaking, he walked away, and Molly didn't even get a chance to reply. She sat watching him go and re-playing what he'd said. Was she over thinking or did he sound like he knew something. Molly shrugged and shook her head. He was just trying to reassure her. That's all.

33 – Ria – 16/06/1996

Ria hadn't tried anything the day before. She wanted Jasper to relax. The more relaxed he was, the less likely he would be to scrutinise her every move. Jasper had been next to her again when she awoke and she played her part well when his eyes eventually opened. She was becoming better at being who he wanted her to be, which was helpful, but also terrified her. If she played this role too long, would she forget who she really was?

Jasper didn't leave until lunchtime. She called it lunchtime, but he hadn't given her any food so far that day. She had begun to get used to his routine. When he went out, it was normally for several hours at a time. When she heard the crunch of gravel as he left in the car, Ria used her teeth on the cable tie around her right wrist. Any pulling on the left one still caused a shooting pain up her wrist. Ria bit hard on the cable tie. She tried initially on the main body of it, before deciding to try the snap joint instead. She bit repeatedly at differing angles, desperate for something to work. It seemed like she'd been biting at her home-made handcuffs for an hour or so before suddenly she heard a snap, and the tether on her right hand fell away. Now she knew she needed to finish the job. If he found her half out again, she dreaded what he would do, either to her or Marc. She managed to snap the second cable tie almost instantly and didn't even pause a moment before jumping from the bed and running from the room. She quickly glanced in the other rooms to satisfy herself that Marc wasn't there, but she hadn't expected him to be. She suspected he wouldn't have been given such a nice prison.

Hammering down the stairs, Ria felt the weakness of her legs from her lack of food or movement for the last few days. Her right hand clung tightly to the banister as she continued.

Ria opened a door in the hallway and saw the steps leading down to the basement where she'd been kept originally. Every cell in her body screamed at her not to go back in, but she couldn't leave if Marc might be there. She stepped down slowly, but steadily. Now she was moving again, she wanted to check and get out. Peering into the room at the bottom of the stairs, it was clear the basement had been turned into a storeroom. It was as if she'd never been there. She raced back up the stairs, bare feet cold as they paced through the house. She moved through the kitchen to the back door and bolted from the house.

Her legs pumped faster than they ever had before. A large barn loomed to her left and although she wanted to get far, far away, she had an inkling Marc could be there. She hadn't found him in the house.

The barn door was bolted with a large plank of semi rotten wood. Ria heaved it up and threw it to the floor. Before she'd even crossed the threshold she could hear it. Quiet moaning or muffled screaming. She marched forward, fearful but determined. Her feet were still bare, and every stone and piece of debris snagged her soles, but she grimaced against the pain and continued.

At one time they must have fixed vehicles in this vast and cluttered barn as there was a pit on the floor, now covered with huge heavy sheets of wood. At the edges, these were weighed down with a variety of cans, tubs and even machines.

Kneeling close to the edge, Ria knew this was the source of the sounds. 'Marc, Marc, is that you?' she tried to project in a loud whisper.

No audible response, so slowly and carefully, Ria began to heave all the objects placed as weights. It was a difficult job, barefoot in the dirt but slowly she found she'd completely uncovered one of the two boards in place. She found it harder to move than she expected.

She persisted in heaving and pivoting it sideways until a space of around one foot was clear and she was sitting in a cloud of dust, tasting the damp decay of the place. A huddled shape shivered at the bottom of the pit, seemingly unaware of her proximity. Silence. Just for a moment, the person stopped moaning and Ria tried again. This time, when she said his name, the head of the person in the pit turned. The person's arms were tied with yet more cable ties to a ring on the floor. He was so filthy it was hard to tell if he had something over his head but as she looked closer, she realised it was just filth. The figure was sat in 6 inches of dirty water, shaking and broken looking. Ria was confident it was Marc. She'd have stopped to save anyone from this place, but she was relieved it was Marc. She called out again gently and the head swung in her direction, his eyes, beacons shining through the dirt.

Ria looked around her until she saw an old crate. Rushing to it and dragging it back, she dropped it into the hole next to where Marc lay. She grabbed an old Stanley knife that sat on a shelf. It was dirty and rusted but would still cut if needed. Next, she slowly lowered herself until she was crouched on the crate, wincing at the pain in her hand, but determined that she would not cry out when he was in such a state. 'Don't step down, there's broken glass everywhere.' The voice was weak and croaky, almost a stranger',s compared to her boyfriend's of mere days ago.

She didn't waste time on words and reassurance, that would come later. She went straight to work on the knots about his wrists. They were tightly applied cable ties, and she struggled to get the knife under them to cut, without slitting his wrists. Then with a movement that caused Ria to fall backwards, the tie snapped open. Ria shuffled forward and Marc began to weep. 'He wasn't going to let me go Ria, he was going to leave me to die like this. Are you really here?'

Through his tears and relief, Ria helped him to his feet, practically dragging him. 'We only have minutes before he's going to start looking for me. Quick.'

With that, Ria climbed on the crate and hauled herself out of the pit. 'Marc, come on, we can talk later, but we need to go. Come on, please be quick.'

Marc hauled himself up easily enough once he'd shaken himself and Ria was relieved, she didn't think she'd be able to lift him. They sprinted for the door. 'Come on, it's that way to the cliffs, we can follow them to town. If we go to the road, he'll find us.'

They squeezed slowly from the barn door and looked around. There was no sign yet that Jasper had noticed Ria's absence, but Ria knew that could change at any moment. She ran, Marc's hand clutched in her own, running towards the cliffs. Just before the main cliff edge was a deep hollow. Ria stopped in time to stop Marc falling straight over the edge. She let go of his hand and knelt to look over the edge. It was full of sea water, pulsating in time with the waves outside this enclosure. They were about to turn East, where they thought the town lay, when a voice barked at them 'Come back now. Ria, how could you do this to me? Ria, this gun is aimed at him. If you care about him at all, you'd better come back now.'

Ria stood, taking hold of Marc's hand again and looking at him. Without speaking, she hoped he understood what her eyes darting sideways meant. Before Jasper could say another word, Ria had spun them both round and they leapt into the swirling waters below. The drop was around twenty-five feet and at the bottom they crashed through the waves into the murky darkness. Ria emerged, looking around in panic until the bewildered face of her exhausted boyfriend appeared too. 'You can't get out of there. There's nowhere to go!' Ria heard Jasper shouting, he'd obviously caught up. Looking up, she saw his smirking face. He was visibly happy that his prisoners had been caught in another trap. Ria initially feared he would shoot them like fish in a barrel, but his head disappeared, and she caught her breath.

Reality hit Ria like a freight train. Looking around her new enclosure, panic began to set in. The walls were sheer it was unlikely either of them would manage to climb out. If they did, Jasper would be waiting at the top. Ria knew that they wouldn't be able to tread water indefinitely, particularly after a few days of almost no food or water.

Ria had regained her equilibrium and was now treading water and looking all around her. 'Marc, tilt your head back a little and try and relax, there's got to be a way out. I'll dive down, look for any other way out. I can feel the pull of the tide so it must connect somewhere.'

Marc slowly leaned back. He was not as comfortable in the water as she was. Ria noticed him expelling much more energy than her by thrashing his arms and legs around more vigorously than was necessary. Ria saw him nod however he seemed to try to conserve more energy. Ria inhaled deeply and then slid under the water smoothly. It didn't take long for her to emerge. 'Nothing, I'll go again.'

Down she went a second time, this time when she emerged, she didn't speak, just shook her head and took a few steadying breaths before going again.

'I think I saw something, but I had to come up for air.' She spluttered her words, she was beginning to feel cold with exhaustion but felt determined to get out of this trap and not sit and wait for Jasper.

'Just breathe for a minute Ria, don't rush it or you'll drown yourself. Here, let me support you for a minute, relax and breathe before you go again.'

Ria complied and lay back, her head supported by Marc and allowed her breathing to settle. She didn't wait for more than thirty seconds before she bolted upright again, ready to dive once more. Ria dived down again and explored the area she thought might hold a tunnel or outlet. She swam through a space in the rock until her lungs were burning and then popped up in a small but very high cave. She waited a moment, regaining her breath and doing a quick reconnaissance on the new cave. If it was a dead end, there was no point in getting Marc to swim to it. It was very high with daylight streaming through the top. When Ria dived down, she felt an exit tunnel and surfaced, ready to return to Marc and bring him through.

It was around five minutes by the time Ria resurfaced to a teary-faced Marc. 'There's a cave, I think there's a way out. Sorry, I had to pause there and get my breath back'

Marc collapsed in sobs, overcome for a moment. 'Will I be able to do it?'

'Yeah, I'll help you. It's not far. You head down right there and then you can use the rocks to pull you if that's easier? The tunnel is only about two meters and as soon as you're out of it, you come up to the surface. There's a ledge in there so you can get out of the water and rest too.'

Marc nodded but crinkled his forehead as he worried about how to manage it. 'I struggle to get down. What if I can't get to the entrance of the tunnel?'

Ria paused a moment, looking with her mind's eye at the journey she'd already taken. 'It's not too far down, I can help you. I'll get you down, then you go through the tunnel. I may have to come back up here for air, then I'll follow you through. Trust me, you can do it.'

Ria got close to Marc then, looking into his eyes, providing the reassurance he seemed to need. They nodded to each other and Ria held up three fingers. She dropped one, then two and when she dropped the third finger, she and Marc inhaled a huge breath and then dived downwards. Ria pulled at Marc's hand, bringing him with her. It wasn't easy as his body seemed to want to stay on the surface, but she persevered and dragged him with her. When they reached the entrance to the tunnel, Ria guided his hands to rocks he could hold and pushed him forward into the space before him. Marc continued and Ria shot back to the surface, spluttering. The exertion of pulling Marc and getting him into position had caused her to expel more breath than she'd wanted to as she grunted and pulled. At the surface, she prayed Marc had made it through and tried to level her breathing to go again.

Just as she was about to dive, she saw a shape dropping down from above. Jasper. She dived down and away, hoping he would not see where they'd gone.

She did it and within minutes she had passed through the tunnel and emerged into the cave, with daylight shining in above and Marc lounging back on a rock shelf, smiling at the achievement. 'He's right behind us, we need to go again'. Ria shouted. 'I'll check out the route first.' Ria was desperate, she knew if Jasper caught her, she would need to either go back or die. There was no other choice available.'

34 – DI Phil Campbell – 16/06/1996

DI Phil Campbell was like a dog with a bone on this kind of investigation. A young woman missing was a ticking clock. If they didn't find her soon, there'd be almost no hope of finding her alive. Even now, the likelihood of a happy ending was slim at best. Phil had spoken to the council and knew that the fluorescent vest-wearing workers in the town centre were from the local dog rescue charity, Barks and Tails.

The tone on the phone rang as Phil Campbell waited for the charity to answer. After around seven rings a bright and young sounding voice answered, a cacophony of barking echoing down the line.

'Hello, I'm Detective Inspector Phil Campbell calling from the police. I urgently need to know the names of the workers that have been out canvassing for you on the high street this week.'

'I think I'll need to speak to my manager for that' answered the young voice.

After establishing that the manager was onsite, Phil asked the woman to give the request to her manager and that he would be down to speak to her in twenty minutes. It was so easy to get fobbed off on the phone and now Phil knew there were people at the offices, he was off. He grabbed a file containing CCTV stills from his desk and booked out a car. He practically jumped down the back stairs and out of the station, where his preferred pool car was parked in a side street.

Even as he drove, Phil Campbell scanned every face he passed, slowed down to check when he saw what appeared to be a homeless person. He was doing no harm and wasn't who he was looking for, so Phil moved on.

When he reached the shelter, just outside of town, he drove up a longer than standard driveway to the back of a large old house that had been converted at some point in its history.

When Phil got out of the car, he scanned, turning in a vast circle on the spot; something was making him feel uneasy. Shrugging it off after finding no reason for it, he rapped on the large double doors of the shelter. It seemed to take a long time before anyone answered, at which point, Phil's hand was raised ready to hammer again, even louder.

'No need detective' smiled an older woman in green medical trousers and a hoody.

She opened one half of the door wide, and Phil slid inside behind her. 'I presume you got my message then? Have you got the details?'

The woman smiled over her shoulder and led him deeper into the building and into a room that looked likely to function as the office. On the large desk were several files, organised in two piles.

'I'm Maggie Ownes, I run this rescue centre. At this time of year, we have lots of volunteers, often students on their travels needing to earn a few quid. They're in two piles, the first is those who worked during the week but only for a day or a few hours, the second pile is those that worked more than three days, some are regulars, some not. What information is it you need?

'Do you know them all? Can you identify them? If I showed you a photo, could you identify him?'

Phil asked, drawing a photograph from his file and placing it on the table, next to the files.

'Oh, well I don't know them all, but I know him. Jasper Stone. He's here for the summer, so has worked with us for a few weeks. Will probably be off in another week or two.'

'Ok great. Can I look at his file? I'll also need a list of all the others, but I suspect it is Jasper we need to speak to.'

'He can't be in trouble surely. He's a lovely lad. I'll get the list sorted. This is Jasper's file. I think... ah yes, we were waiting for him to confirm where he's staying. He said he was house-sitting and was due to update us. I presume he never got back to us. There's a number for him there though.'

Phil Campbell rapidly made the most urgent notes and could see a photocopy of a passport. 'Are you able to copy this information for me?'

Maggie nodded, taking the file and disappearing behind another door, where the sound of a photocopier being brought back to life filled the room.

After Phil had gleaned all the information he could, he left and headed back to the station. There was progress; he now knew the identity of the other suspect and they could begin to track him down. The phone number was for a landline and was not local. It was from somewhere in Oxfordshire from the looks of it, so unlikely to be where Jasper was at present, but they would do some research before calling it.

The office had been relatively quiet when he left, still early for some, but when he returned, it was bustling in every corner. She'd been gone six days and things were not looking good. Phil was happy to walk in with something that could move the investigation forward, even if it wasn't as much as he would like.

'Team, listen in. The Manager at the dog rescue place identified him. It's a match. His name is Jasper Stone. Apparently this guy is house-sitting for an old couple, don't know the address yet. Charlie, can your team please get on that – any local house-sits, or short-term lets that stand out.'

'Have you checked notice boards in town? I'm sure I saw an advert on there yesterday. The board by the town hall. Get an officer to take a look, will you? It might be nothing but worth checking.' Charlie Knight was a grizzly detective sergeant who seemed to object to any tasks being given to him.

'Let me know how you get on with that Charlie' the detective inspector replied. He should have volunteered in the first place.

***

A young female officer ran into the Major Investigations office. 'I've got an address. Just down the coast from where the girl was taken, probably a ten-minute drive at most. It's the Glamcoe's farm. They're a lovely old couple, I often speak to them on patrols because they're out of the way and their family have all moved away now. I checked the notice board and when I saw it was them, it all clicked. They told me a young man was house-sitting for six weeks over the summer and that they were staying with family in Kent. I phoned them. They've given me their son's number in case there were any issues while they were away. I spoke to them and it's him, Jasper Stone, that is house-sitting. I didn't tell them anything else, but they'd appreciate an update later, I'm sure.'

'Ah thank you, that is just what I needed to hear! Pc...?'

'Anderson sir. Tina Anderson. Do you need anything else, or shall I leave you all to it?'

'That's all and thank you. I may get in touch if we need to contact the Glamcoe's again, but if you could leave their contact details anyway.' With that, DI Campbell turned to his team. 'Get your teams mobilised and Charlie, get the briefing ready for one o'clock.' He barked at his detective sergeants and exhaled, allowing his shoulders to relax just a little. It wasn't over but he was so relieved to have a lead, it felt like he'd won the lottery. Heading to his office via the canteen, he sat down with a coffee and panini, anticipating a long afternoon.

35 – Jasper – 16/06/2025

Jasper had enjoyed coffee with one of the friends, Molly earlier in the day and kept thinking back to it. Enjoying her sad eyes and hopelessness. He'd been out in the town and had seen her looking sad and lost and followed her into the café. He was wearying of this town and the charade and beginning to look forward to their next destination and his and Ria's new life together.

He drove back out of town and to the farm that was home for now. The car was steady and reliable, just like the Glamcoe's he'd borrowed it from. When the time came to leave, he would need to sort out new number plates so they could keep the car.

As Jasper drove up the long driveway, he looked up to the window of the room where he kept Ria and smiled. Soon he'd find her waving out of the window for him, having waited patiently for his return. Soon, but not quite yet. She was being amenable, but he knew she was intelligent, he didn't want to believe her until he was certain she loved him as he loved her.

When he parked and stepped up to the house, he opened the front door smiling. As he stepped over the thresh-hold however, he knew something wasn't right. Closing the door behind him, it slammed. He must have left a window or door open, he thought, despite being certain he hadn't.

He immediately sprinted up the stairs but hesitated before opening the door to Ria's room, dread leaching through his veins that it might have happened again.

Gently twisting the door handle, he flung the door wide and dropped to his knees at the sight of the empty bed. A visceral moan erupted from his lips and tears sprung from his eyes. It took a moment for him to get himself together again and he stood, draining the emotion from his face and swallowing down the feelings of betrayal and abandonment that so often haunted him.

Moving into the neighbouring bedroom and sliding to the floor, he stretched his arm under the bed and withdrew a shotgun. The Glamcoe's had left it locked in the gun cabinet, but Jasper had quickly found the key and moved for convenience.

As Jasper reached the top of the landing, he saw through the window, two figures in the distance, moving quickly. Ria and Marc had escaped. She'd saved him, which meant she'd lied to Jasper. It had all been lies.

Jasper ran from the house, a glance at the barn showed the doors flung wide and an escape hole from the pit. Jasper ran hard. They hadn't looked back for a little while and he didn't think they'd seen him. He hoped he could make up some ground before they did.

They were heading straight for the collapsed sea cave that Jasper had seen on his first day at the farmhouse. They had nowhere to go and despite running hard, he felt the stress levels in his body calming. He would get them back, or perhaps, he would get her back. The boy would need to go. It had been a good idea to start with, but it had over complicated things in the end.

Finally, Jasper was within one hundred feet of his quarry, and he watched as they both stopped. They must have reached the cave. Jasper hitched his shotgun into place, ready to shoot if he had to.

Ria looked behind her and Jasper saw notes of recognition on her face as she looked at him. 'Come back now. Ria, how could you do this to me? Ria, this gun is aimed at him, if you care about him at all, you'd better come back now.' Jasper had screamed the words before he'd even thought about it. He really wanted an excuse to shoot Marc now that he was back in the daylight.

Before Jasper could pull the trigger, he saw Ria and Marc disappear over the edge, jumping potentially to their deaths.

Jasper ran, panting to the edge and looked down at their heads bobbing above the surface of the water. 'You can't get out of there. There's nowhere to go!' he shouted which caused him to relax. It was true, there was no way out. He would need to get a rope to haul Ria out, but she was stuck until he was ready. Smiling, Jasper headed back towards the barn to get rope. He didn't intend to hurry; she deserved a little discomfort for this escape attempt. She would need more later too, that was certain.

When Jasper approached the barn, his stride was wide, his arms swinging. Now the fear of escape was over, he was looking forward to the evening. He wanted Ria to choose to be with him after all this, but he didn't mind using punishment at times to get there. It had been a little dull while she'd been behaving so well.

A sound drew Jasper's attention to the house. The sound was of vehicles crunching on gravel. Vehicles. More than one. A flash of blue light reflected on a wall and Jasper knew it was time to go. He ran to the cliffs, intending to climb down and escape along the coast but as he reached the collapsed cave, he noticed that Marc was gone, and Ria looked up at him. Without thinking further, he flung himself forward into the water. When he returned to the surface, Ria was gone. There was a way out after all.

It took several dives and spluttered returns to the surface with Jasper looking up each time. Once he'd found the entrance, he looked up one last time to see police gathering at the point from which he'd jumped. He dived down and swam through, adrenaline coursing through him but also hope. He wasn't far from her now.

37 – DI Phil Campbell – 16/06/1996

Just before one 'o'clock, DI Campbell headed down to the briefing room, sitting at the back and letting DS Charlie Knight take to the floor. The room held a projector at the front and space enough to seat about forty. DI Campbell looked around as he sat down; he liked to be familiar with those going on a job like this with him. There were two detective sergeants he knew well, including Charlie Knight and six additional detective constables. There were also a further six uniformed officers, radios blaring distractingly every few minutes, sitting together to one side.

'I think that's everyone so let's get going. This' Charlie Knight pointed at the large projector screen beside him, 'is Jasper Stone. He is twenty-three years old and is staying on a farm, here.' Here, Charlie changed the slide to show a map of the area. DI Campbell enjoyed watching his cocky façade when he briefed the less-experienced officer. He knew how much Charlie wanted his job, he wasn't getting it yet though. 'The yellow star is the location Ria Roe was last seen, red is the farmhouse and orange is our rendez-vous point or RVP. Less than a ten-minute drive to the red dot which is Stone's temporary home. Intel on this is minimal, we think he has a fake identity and therefore, presume he is high risk'.

'There are no other residents we are aware of but it's a substantial property so expect anything. Be aware, he's cuckooed himself here while house-sitting, a lot of the property will belong to the owners, look for what sticks out. The helicopter has had a quick run across for us with thermal imaging. The imaging would be better at night, but it has given us enough for now. There seems to be an outbuilding out on the West side. With that in mind, expect secret hide-outs, tunnels, anything. I'm hoping Stone will be there and we can arrest him quickly, I want to take our time with the search. We will be searching for information in any form on the abduction of Ria Roe. We will be seizing electronics, any relevant paperwork. I want everyone to be very forensically aware. Shoe coverings for everyone and overalls once the initial arrest has been made. Any questions?'

With that, DI Phil Campbell watched as the detective Sergeant scanned the faces in front of him. 'I've got the warrant' the detective inspector added.

'Great, the forensic team is on standby. Ambulance service knows what's happening and have a crew on standby. Let's do this.'

With that, the room erupted in moving bodies. Chairs scraping, a murmur of voices and the crinkly noise of waterproof jackets being drawn over body armour, followed by heavy boots stomping away and heading to their vehicles. The detective inspector missed being a constable on jobs like this. He missed getting stuck in rather than overseeing everyone else.

When the briefing room was empty, the senior officer nodded to his detective sergeants. They were ready. Leaving the room, DI Campbell drew a determined look on his face 'Let's bring that poor girl home. Come on'. With that, they left the station and the hunt was on.

The RVP or rendezvous point was in a dip in the road, invisible from the property. The troops gathered and then all sped forward, one after the other, tearing into the courtyard with a roar of engines and a screech of brakes. Officers scattering to cover rear doors and windows.

It took moments before the first uniformed officers were hammering at the front door with their *big red key* or enforcer; a handheld battering ram used to put doors in at speed. The third hit smashed the front door half off its hinges. The officers at the front plunged in, fully expecting for Stone to have made off already, which was readily confirmed. Several shouts of 'CLEAR' rang through the house until DI Campbell was satisfied. 'Move on to the grounds, I'll take a look around the house'.

The stomp of heavy boots slowly faded, and DI Campbell walked slowly through the house, getting a feel for it and noticing the things that seemed incongruous. When he opened the front bedroom door, it was clear that he was in the right place. Ropes, cable ties and a lack of anything much else besides the bed. He leaned out of the room and into the neighbouring bedroom which was decorated in the fashion of twenty years prior and full of knick-knacks and memories.

There was a bag on the floor and Phil thought back to all the reports he'd read. An over-sized green rucksack with several keyrings hanging on it. He was certain it was Ria's and now the question remained, where was she and was she still alive.

The smell of salt and seaweed was strong in the cave, accompanied by the echoing crash of waves. The snippet of blue sky above provided all the hope they needed. 'I think I can climb it. I nearly choked on that last swim, I'm not sure I could do it again.' Marc spoke as Ria was preparing to dive again but instead heaved herself from the water.

'Are you kidding? It looks impossible. I don't think I could. I don't think I have the strength, and my left hand is pretty mangled, although thankfully less painful with the cold water. I was going to explore the other tunnel. He'll be right behind us, there's no time to figure out the best way.'

Ria's brow furrowed as she looked up, feeling nauseous at the thought of climbing up there.

'I don't think I can do another tunnel. If it comes out in the sea I might drown, I'm not a great swimmer Ria. I can climb and get help, you wait here.' Marc looked up with hope not fear. He had confidence in his skills, despite his recent malnutrition.

Marc stood and Ria kissed him, slowly and deeply. Imbuing every ounce of her feelings for him into one moment. Then, he began the slow ascent up the perilous rock face without a rope or any protection.

Ria watched for several minutes until Marc was out of sight and well on his way out of their current prison. Ria had pulled off a neck scarf that Jasper had given her and threw it on the ledge in the cave. Ria was not going to wait here, she wanted to get out, now. She took a deep breath and forced herself down. As she submerged, she almost thought she saw someone in the water next to her. She continued, hoping that she was just hallucinating, but with a sneaking suspicion she was trying to ignore, that it was Jasper, close behind her. Ria swam on. If it was him, she needed to move quickly. It was then that she felt fingers grabbing at her ankle. Kicking out, her heal connected with something and she swam on. Terror forced bubbles of air from her mouth as her arms and legs tried to thrust her forward towards the light ahead. Stars erupted and her lungs felt ready to implode, desperate for a gulp of air. Her arms had begun to slow down as she felt her empty lungs draining the energy from her body.

She reached the surface gasping and sucking in huge lungfuls of oxygen. Terror still filled her as she swam out, away from the cliff, seaweed swiping at her legs, imitations of Jaspers grip but no less terrifying.

As her heart rate began to steady, her breathing became more relaxed. Treading water, she looked back at the small rocky cove she'd swam from and could see no identifiable signs of whereabouts she was and no signs yet of Jasper. Scanning the cliffs and land closest to her, her eyes were drawn by an angry looking seagull swooping and diving before it eventually settled on a ledge. She could see no sign of Marc and was unsure where precisely he would have emerged but hopefully this meant he was already on his way to raise the alarm.

Invigorated by her escape, despite hunger and exhaustion, Ria still felt the pressure of pursuit and swam out to sea a little further, avoiding the smattering of rocks in the water where she'd emerged. She stopped there and watched a while longer. Nobody emerged and she blinked away the salt water from her eyes along with her fears that he was still after her, even now. She began swimming West, towards the now setting sun, desperate for a reunion with her friends, family and of course, her boyfriend. She'd decided in that dark cave, if she got out, WHEN she got out, she would not hide herself in the shadows ever again. Marc should never have been a secret, and she could no longer remember why she thought he should be in the first place.

Ria dragged herself from the water, up the sandy beach and towards the lights that were beginning to spring to life, desperate to see someone. Anyone.

Halfway up the beach she collapsed. Her cheek resting on the sand, the scratchiness feeling sharp to her exhausted body. Rolling onto her back, she looked up at darkening velvet sky and breathed deep, her freedom hitting her, as tears began to flood her face. It had been at least a few days, she knew that but was unclear what day it was or if her friends would still be nearby. She desperately wanted to fall into friendly arms and handover the baton of survival to them.

A dark figure approached from the promenade and Ria curled in on herself, fear overtaking her once again, knowing she had nothing left to fight with. As the figure turned to look at her, the light glinted on his face and she recognised Nathan, a lad they'd met while drinking a lifetime ago. 'Ria' he barked, causing her to draw back.

'I'm not gonna hurt you, Ria. The police, they're everywhere, they've been looking for you, everyone has.' He extended a hand at this, and Ria's body slowly unfurled, her hand slipping into his as he heaved her to her feet. Staggering forwards, she leant her weight into Nathans solid frame, Ria walked towards the light and back towards her life.

'I'm sorry I was so pushy before. I didn't mean to upset you'. Nathan was looking at her, sincerity in his voice.

Nathan's behaviour seemed like a lifetime ago and Ria couldn't even begin to process his words. She just kept moving forward.

PART THREE

Ria felt overwhelmed as she shuffled into town, supported by Nathan. The food smells ushering from the busy restaurants made her salivate and realise how hungry she was. When the police realised who she was, they swooped in, radios blasting and sat her in a car, on top of a paper bag, it crinkled as she sat down and was less than comfortable. Too many voices were trying to speak to her, and too many faces were looking in. She finally felt the utter exhaustion that had been threatening. Eventually, an older police officer looked at her, spoke quietly to her, but his words were lost in the melee. The officer then gently closed the door of the police car and he and his colleague got inside. Once all the doors were shut, it felt like being under water, there was still lots of noise, but it was diffused. Ria was driven away, watching the faces light up blue and red. The noise slowly petered out. Ria arrived at the police station within minutes, she felt safe in the car and almost unwilling to leave it now, but as the door opened, she acquiesced. Ria heaved herself up the steps to the front door held open for her and stepped inside. The blank, bleak walls felt like they were closing in on her, a mixture of trauma and exhaustion leaving her depleted. She was left to sit in a side room, alone, terrified and absolutely overwhelmed. Her parents were shown in about twenty minutes later and she collapsed into her mum's arms, awkward and still, while her dad looked on.

After several minutes, Ria pulled herself up to sitting, her Mum holding her hand, while Ria explained what she could to the police officer that had shown her parents in and then lingered. The suited police officer was very keen to know about her escape, where she went and how many small caves she had to traverse. It later became clear, through overheard, whispered conversations that they'd lost him. Her kidnapper had escaped into the caves, and they were yet to find him.

Sat in the stuffy interview room, Ria had been speaking slowly, methodically, telling her story but now her eyes raised to the detective. 'Where's Marc? I thought he'd be here.'

The detective, who had introduced himself as Phil squirmed. 'Nobody has seen him. Could he have been involved in taking you? Were they working as a team?'

'Marc was absolutely not involved and if you haven't seen him, you need to start searching because he was climbing out of one of the caves. We were together. He was going to get help! That psycho Jasper took us both!'

Tears streamed down her face, Ria struggled to still the shake in her hands. She was safe now, but she knew it wasn't over. She wouldn't relax until they caught him. She'd presumed that Marc had been found by someone else and that he'd turn up at any moment. But now, devastation eked through her cells as she realised there was every chance that Marc was trapped or hurt and that maybe he hadn't made it out.

'Please. Please find him.' She whispered, to the retreating back of the detective.

The search of the house had provided much in the way of forensic material and other evidence. Jasper had been seen by officers jumping into a collapsed sea cave. The manhunt was now on.

Detective Inspector Phil Campbell briefed the search teams from a café on the beach he'd temporarily taken over. A large map of the area was spread out on the sticky tables. 'Alpha team, here' he said as he circled an area of cliffs and caves that were right on the sea and at sea level.

'Bravo team, the upper cliffs here.'

Bravo team area nudged up to the Alpha team area but covered the higher ground and clifftops.

'Charlie team here, Delta team here'.

The final two teams covered the potential entry and exits points for the area.

'Please ensure you all have your personal protective equipment and take your individual team briefings shortly, based on the terrain. Be safe and let's find this bastard.'

The teams were not as big as Phil would have liked, but resources were short. He'd requested support from neighbouring counties, but it was yet to arrive, and any delay might mean the escape of their suspect.

After a few questions, the team checked their kit, and began the task at hand, the manhunt for Jasper Stone. About thirty minutes after moving out, the police radio clasped in DI Campbell's hand exploded into life. 'DI Campbell from 685 Team Alpha. Respond.'

'Go ahead Alpha.'

'We have found the cave entrance and it's secured, awaiting equipment to explore within.'

'Acknowledged, update when available.'

'Gov, 179 Team Beta here, we've found someone, deceased. There's a lot of blood, but I think it's the Frenchman. On top of the cliffs, close to a small tunnel leading into the caves. No sign of the suspect. Scene secured. There will be access for scene of crime officers if they go past the rendezvous point and up to the viewpoint. If they radio once they're there I'll come and meet them to show the safest route.'

'That's acknowledged Beta.' Phil Campbell looked to the sky, hoping for inspiration to come. He had suspected Marc might be dead, but he dreaded breaking it to that poor young woman who had already been through so much. Sweat pooled in the small of his back and heat began creeping up his neck along with the fear that Stone might have slipped through the net.

***

Hours flew by with various messages being passed back and forth, but still no suspect located. Jasper Stone seemed to have vanished. The search teams were eventually re-distributed in a wider arc around the original site, but no trace of Jasper Stone was found. His image was sent to the local bus companies, train companies, taxis and an alert was put out for him on the police national computer.

Phil Campbell didn't want to give Ria any bad news. He wanted to walk in and say he'd arrested the man that took her while ushering in her boyfriend. The disappointment leached through his veins, adding a heaviness to his demeanour.

She'll never move on if he's not caught Phil thought, desperately trying to think of something he'd missed. He'd tasked several officers to review CCTV for the relevant times. Jasper's car was being watched by a covert officer and hadn't been touched since he escaped. Jasper's phone was now firmly in the possession of the police, with a specialist officer interrogating it. Jasper's temporary home and known associate's addresses were being watched, but so far, they had nothing. His associates were new acquaintances in any case; people he'd befriended in the last couple of weeks. Nobody seemed to have known him longer. He'd clearly come from elsewhere, Phil just had to figure out where.

He stepped slowly and reluctantly into his car, there was nothing more he could do at present. He needed to speak to Ria.

42 – Callie – 17/06/1996

They'd had a call the night before. Ria had been found. The police had told Callie that Ria was fine but would not be able to see them until the following day.

The night had been long and unsettled but the day had now arrived, and they were expecting Ria at any moment. Callie sat between her friends on the old sofa. She wasn't usually one for hugging, but they'd been sat huddled together for the last hour. Silent and unsure. Ria had been found, but what on earth had she been through? Callie felt like a different person from a week previously and Ria would have been affected a million times more.

Callie felt herself shrinking. Unsure of what she would say when Ria finally arrived. Should they ask her what happened or just get on with getting home and returning to their normal lives?

The sound of the door opening brought Callie from her reflections. She jumped from her seat and felt almost ready to vomit now that the time had come. Mrs Roe stepped into the room, followed by Ria. She was pale and drawn and her eyes seemed to dart around more than they ever had before. Molly stepped in front of Callie and put her arms around Ria, Olivia followed suit. Callie hesitated a moment, it felt uncomfortable to her, but she leant in and enclosed her three friends in an embrace.

'It's alright. I'll be alright'. Ria's muffled voice crept out from under the enclosure of friendship.

Callie almost felt a collective exhale. A relief that if Ria said that things would be alright, that eventually their worlds would settle down and become as they had been. Full of laughter rather than pain.

Callie had released her friends and Molly and Olivia had gently released Ria too. Molly still clasped her hand though.

'I don't want to talk about it. I'm heading home with

mum and dad in a bit, and we wanted to check you could still get back on another coach. I would wait but I really need to go back to hospital, and I'd rather do it back home.' Ria didn't make eye contact. She seemed like she was in some sort of daze, going through the motions but not really present. Callie didn't blame her.

Silence fell. Callie was usually the chatty one but had no idea what to say. Eventually Molly spoke. 'I'll sort the coach, don't worry about us. Just look after yourself and we'll see you back home. I'm glad you're safe Ria.' Molly hugged her again when she stopped speaking, tears tracing down her cheeks. She was always better at embracing emotions than Callie.

Mrs Roe had been silent until then but moved towards Ria. 'We'd better go. Your dad's waiting in the car.'

With that, Ria and her mum slowly left.

Callie stood on the doorstep with Molly and Olivia waving them off. Once out of sight, a sense of dread filled Callie's gut. Ria may have said she's alright, but maybe she never would be?

43 - Jasper – 17/06/1996

Jasper had been on the move for years now, always finding places stay. He had the face that encouraged trust with his large brown eyes and floppy hair. His accent, just short of posh but well-bred enough to make people feel they could trust him.

He found the holiday season perfect. There were always jobs to do and in the busiest seaside towns, some of the residents left for the peak of the season, unwilling to tolerate the hordes of tourists that would inevitably take over.

Jasper had found it easy enough to create some fake identification, when you seemed trustworthy, people would accept almost anything.

He'd been shocked today, it had been far too close. He could still feel the buffeting waves, dragging him across the rocks, the suffocating saltwater seeping into his lungs; the sea had nearly taken him. Even now, several miles away his skin itched with nerves and a deep-seated anger that things had not gone to plan. He sat amongst trees, on the outside of a campsite, just North of St Afan. He watched a man, woman and two children as they laughed and played and finally zipped up their tent before they loaded up their car and drove away. Presumably, a day of sight-seeing was ahead of them. The man was in his early thirties and around five foot nine or ten inches tall and medium build. His clothes would be perfect. Jasper assessed as he watched, also looking beyond the tent at the rest of the site to what else he might make use of. As more families began to mill about, he decided he would need to be cautious, grabbing only essentials.

Jasper crept forward and slipped into the tent, eyes scanning the stuffy space to find the right bag. A large blue rucksack stood neatly to the side of the entrance and Jasper knelt, the crinkly ground sheet loud in the early morning stillness. Reaching in he smiled, men's clothing that would likely work for him. He quickly changed, leaving his damp clothes in a pile. Once dressed, he took a few other supplies and after emptying the rucksack, stuffed his swag deeply within. He found a carrier bag, wrapped his own clothes in it and then added that to the bag. Swinging it onto his back, he poked a furtive head out of the tent flap, before extracting himself, zipping up the tent and then striding back into the treeline.

He now had supplies, clothes and food, enough to make it several miles on foot until he was far enough away to come up with a new plan. He was unclear whether the girl had made it out. He thought he would catch up with her, but he hadn't done. Perhaps there were more tunnels than he'd realised. With any luck, she'd have been stuck down there and not emerge at all. Once he was a safe distance, he would try a pub and see if he could catch the news.

The sound of sirens had screeched through the air at several points as Jasper walked, but none close enough to trouble him. He was walking on the coastal path, rucksack on. His feet were beginning to struggle with blisters due to the boots he'd taken being a size or so too large, but the main thing, the important thing, was that he blended in.

He had fled his temporary home in the late evening and now, marching in the sun the following morning he began to unfurl. He hadn't slept and the sparkles on the water were enough to make him feel dizzy. *Another hour, then a break* he told himself. He couldn't afford to hang around, but he didn't want to be so tired he made mistakes.

Jasper kept walking until he had changed his name, cut his hair and got clothes more akin to surfers than his usual more preppy style. He kept walking into his new life, leaving this mess behind.

44 – Ria – 14/08/1996

Ria had missed the deadline for her final essay, and she'd missed her exams. They were unimportant compared to the trauma she'd endured in Cornwall, but as she stood in the school courtyard waiting for the brown envelope containing her results, she felt the bitter taste of it. She'd worked so hard and now her grades would be determined by guesswork. She could feel the walls of the future she was building, crumbling around her.

Ria stood alone, her friends had agreed to meet her there, but she was not blind to the distance that had grown between them since their ill-fated holiday. Ria knew that she'd changed and the neat little box she used to survive in would no longer hold her. She could no longer laugh at their childish jokes or tolerate Callie's barbed jibes.

She watched as the three people, that she'd spent more time with than anyone else over the last ten years, approached. Callie looking fierce and unconcerned, Molly wearing clothes that gave off serious hippy vibes and Olivia, still looking a little lost and a little on edge, as she often did.

As Ria watched them approach, she felt the crawling up her spine and the tingling that followed. The unmistakable feeling that she was being watched. She tried to shake it off, she was at school after all, there were people everywhere. She couldn't ignore it though and slowly turned a full circle on the spot. She saw nothing unusual. Until with a final glance, she saw a bunch of flowers on a low wall behind her. She stepped closer, nobody else was close enough to lay claim to them. Yellow roses. She remembered when she'd first been speaking to Jasper, he'd told her to talk, and she'd babbled on the best she could. She'd told him how she thought yellow roses were much nicer than the red ones that were usually connected to romance.

Ria slowly slipped the card from a plastic sleeve. When she opened it, she gasped, it felt like a she had been dunked in a bucket of ice. *Ria, I'll ALWAYS love you.*

The world had gone silent for Ria. She was back being caressed by the lunatic in Cornwall. The words in Ria's mind that had been whirling now settled. *He'll never let you go.*

The hands of her friends on her shoulder snapped her back to reality and she hastily dropped the flowers over the wall. He might not want to let her go but she was certain she would do everything she could to rcmove him from her life and her thoughts.

'Ready for you're A star, star, stars Ria?' Callie thought she was funny, she always did these little jokes with no idea of how knotted up Ria's insides were.

'Ha ha, funny' was all Ria could manage as a reply. If Cornwall had been a normal holiday, and she'd taken her exams as planned, she would have been confident of her grades. Surly even Callie could see that this wasn't the case any longer?

'I think we're all a bit worried to be honest Ria.' Molly's ability to empathise always surpassed the others and Ria felt relieved that at least someone understood her turmoil.

Thankfully the doors to the sixth form block were flung open wide and the year head, Mrs Maple stood small in the space. Small in stature but never in the fear she had reigned with throughout their school years. She wore a lot of make-up and sometimes seemed more of a caricature than a real person, but Ria had seen the gentle side behind her fierce exterior. When she returned to school, devastated and broken, Mrs Maple had been a force to be reckoned with, promising to submit grades and do all she could to get the results she said she knew Ria deserved. Ria took a deep breath and hoped Mrs Maple's efforts were enough.

Ria and her friends took their place in the loose queue

created by the throng of students. Ria had barely seen anyone else from school since her abduction and was not immune to the whispers and side eyes she was receiving. She was glad that school in general had prepared her to ignore the opinions of most of her year group. She had always had a small friendship group with little care for most people and their constant attempts to keep up with the 'in' crowd. She had always preferred to be anything but 'in'. She valued her own freedom and autonomy too much to give in to being popular. She knew she went along with her own group a bit, but she always felt she could say no when she wanted to.

Ria looked at her friends' faces. Olivia was a pale shade of green and nibbling quietly on her nails, unable to join in with any chatter. Callie was keeping up an almost constant stream of 'oh god, do you think I've failed? What if I've failed? My mock results were rubbish.' Molly stood listening but apparently taking deep breaths. Ria watched as Molly's eyes wandered across the crowd. She suspected Molly was blocking out Callie's constant dialogue as much as she was trying to.

As those at the front of the queue stepped away with their envelopes, responses varied from smiles to tears to laughter. When the four friends finally reached the front, Ria stayed back, allowing the other three to get their results before her.

When she stepped up, Mrs Maple took her envelope from the table and handed it over. She made eye contact and quietly said 'good luck' in a tone she hadn't really used with the others.

The sweat erupted in Ria's palms as she clutched that envelope, leaving damp prints on the edges. Ria followed her friends to a space away from the throng of students and they all looked at each other. 'Good luck guys, fingers crossed.' Ria said it and received similar comments in response before they all nodded and began opening.

Tearing open the top of the envelope, Ria slipped a lone piece of paper out. She felt the clenched fist that had been gripping her stomach all morning loosen. She'd done it. Or perhaps Mrs Maple had, but either way, she'd got the grades she needed. She was going to Oxford.

Callie's response to looking at her grades was 'not too bad, good job my expectations were not too high!'

Molly smiled peacefully 'I got what I needed for uni. What about you Liv?'

'I actually did better than I expected.' As she spoke, Ria watched her face change. Pride infusing it with a confidence it usually lacked.

Together they began to walk away, time to celebrate on the whole. As they walked, Ria glanced over her shoulder. The flowers she'd dropped behind the wall were just visible peeping out from behind it. She shook her head, refusing to allow him space in her thoughts.

***

With a celebratory beer or two at a local pub, Ria eventually arrived home. It certainly felt like the end of an era and Ria felt content that it was ending as it should, with her about to leap into the unknown and follow her dreams. She didn't really feel like it yet, but she knew things would improve with time.

She opened the door, and her mum welcomed her with a huge hug. This was one change she was still getting used to. Her mum had been so severe before and now she hugged her every chance she got. She'd become kinder in how she spoke to her and Ria curled into the hug appreciating it. 'Three A stars.' Ria was slightly muffled by her mum's shoulder as she said this but felt the resulting extra squeeze as the response.

'Well done, I'm so pleased. You deserve it, you worked hard. Oh, someone left some flowers outside for you, no name on the tag.'

Her mum had begun to move away into the kitchen,

gesturing and Ria froze praying it would not be him. As she stepped into the kitchen the yellow roses were arranged in a tall glass vase. 'They're from him. He's not going to leave me alone, is he?'

Ria watched her mum reach for the phone and call it straight in to the police. She could only hear half the conversation but comments like 'I don't think it's a copycat.' provided Ria with little hope it was going to be taken seriously.

45 – Jasper – 24/10/1996

The warm conservatory caused the sweat to gather on his upper lip, which he licked away periodically. Jasper has found another home to lay low in. This time, he did not go looking for his next love interest. Maybe this time, he needed to see it through.

Jasper spread the newspaper wide on his lap. He'd caught a headline as he was passing the newsstand in the supermarket and decided to look closer. He'd seen snippets on the television news of course but hadn't been certain of the connection. He needed to see it in black and white. The headline was shocking, as they always try to be. *Multiple murder and suicide - Remains of man and several women found in garden of Oxfordshire house.*

Jasper hadn't heard a name yet and began scouring the article to see if one was announced. Around halfway down the article a neighbour from the property was quoted *"I think it's that Dennis Wilson. He lived there many years ago and disappeared suddenly. The council presumed he'd abandoned his tenancy and re-claimed the property. Lovely couple in there now, I bet they're devastated".*

The article continued. *We are yet to receive confirmation of the identity of the bodies but if the deceased male is of Dennis Wilson, we understand he had a child. Investigations so far have failed to locate the child, Neil Wilson who would probably be mid-twenties by now. He is not suspected of involvement, he would only have been a child, but he may be able to shed light on the sad happenings at this very normal-looking suburban home. It seems the mystery will continue. Please get in touch if you know anything about this unfolding situation and the identities of those involved.*

Jasper sat open mouthed. He couldn't remember the address where he'd lived with his dad, but it was in

Oxfordshire. The image accompanying the article sent an icy tendril down his spine.

Once he'd turned eighteen, he'd cut ties with his remaining family and left the area, never looking back. He had never been allowed to ask about his parents, so he'd allowed himself to forget. He'd forgotten it all until he saw the photograph of the house, his house when he was a child. Now, images started the play across his mind. Images from different times in that house and then... images from those last few days. Sounds. Feelings. The absolute horror.

As a detective inspector in a large rural police force, the cases came and went. DI Phil Campbell knew that his time on each case was limited. Especially when the leads had dried up.

He'd found a lot of related evidence since the investigation began and had used one of the walls in the senior CID office to arrange the major parts of the investigation. He gazed at it now, aware it was time to take it down but still resistant. A suspect had been circulated with a list of different names. They hadn't found his actual legal name; it might be any or none of those that they knew.

As the weeks passed, they'd heard of similar situations all around the country, same description as Jasper Stone. The name in each case was different, but the 'modus operandi', or method of operating, was the same. They had a serial abuser and potential killer, and not one of the six police forces involved had a clue who their suspect was. They certainly didn't know where he was. They had fingerprints. They'd been lifted from the farmhouse but even with those, they weren't certain they belonged to him.

DI Campbell had spoken to Ria Roe at intervals. She insisted that Jasper Stone, or whoever he was, had left her flowers on exam results day. She also found flowers in her halls of residence when she started university. Forensics had tried to lift prints, but nothing had been found, and no further leads were open to him.

The detective inspector hated to see someone get away with a crime. Of course it happened, but in a case like this, it was intolerable. He'd been ordered from further up the chain to circulate the suspect and close the case until he was located. The reasoning being that as there were limited resources and even fewer leads, there was no sense in continuing to fixate on the case. They didn't seem to understand that whether the case was open or not was irrelevant, DI Phil Campbell would not be capable of dropping this one.

Most police officers during their years of service have a small number of cases that pierced them deeply. Whether through loss or a lack of closure. DI Campbell had worked on other abduction cases, but they'd always reached some form of resolution. The accused may have got a lighter sentence than deserved, but they'd at least been held to account and convicted. Although the abduction of Ria Roe was relatively recent, Phil knew he would obsess over it until the culprit was caught, with or without the permission of his senior officers.

He slowly unpinned various images of Jasper Stone, or whatever his real name was, off the walls and organised them in a file. When the case had been linked to others, Phil had accessed photos of the other victims. It was clear this man had a type. Phil felt his features morph into a sneer as the adrenaline jumped at the thought of him.

Once he'd packed away the files into neat boxes, stacked and ready for storage, he knew there was one more thing he had to do. He was glad that Ria Roe was now eighteen and he could dispense with updating her parents. He knew he needed to update Ria.

As he listened to the tones of the phone ringing, waiting for Ria to pick up, he wondered how she was coping now, eighteen months on from her ordeal. Did she still keep someone with her wherever she went? Did she go anywhere at all or was she still living her life in virtual hiding?

As Phil had listened to numerous rings, he was preparing to hang up when a gentle voice murmured from the earpiece. 'Hello'.

'Ria, it's Detective Inspector Phil Campbell. How are

you doing?'

'I'm ok I suppose. You know he'll never stop though detective, don't you? He's subtle now, but I know he's still around. I've called the police a million times and I think I'm on their list of crazy callers now. They don't believe a word I say.'

'I believe you Ria. Sadly, unless there's some evidence, I can't do anything. His picture from CCTV has been circulated pretty much everywhere in the country. Do you remember everything I told you about staying safe? Never let your guard down. I'll speak to your local station, try to get them to take it seriously. The thing is Ria, I've been ordered to close the case. Now it's circulated and there are no other leads for me to follow, I have to circulate him as wanted and wait. You can still call me if anything happens. Report it locally first, then give me the reference and details. Then I can check up that the local cops are doing everything they can. I'm sorry, I wish I could do more.'

The silence on the end of the line was deafening and interrupted only by the odd stifled sob. Eventually Ria answered, she sounded like the air had been kicked out of her. 'OK Phil, thanks. I get it, it's fine. Thanks for everything you've done anyway. Bye.'

With that, the call was disconnected and Phil moved forward with the weight of disappointment sitting heavy in his gut. He had to close it, but he would still dive into it as often as he could. The reality was though, he had other cases that were current and needed attention. He just didn't have the resources to keep dragging over the same case indefinitely. As he sealed up the last box and completed the relevant labels, he knew that it was a mistake, but a mistake he had argued about for long enough.

47 - Ria – 10/06/2025

Ria was nervous. She'd spoken to Phil, Detective Inspector Phil Campbell, many times over the years but she'd not seen him in person since 1996. She was wearing a bright red floral sun dress and felt conspicuous as she usually wore more muted tones. When he eventually stepped through the door, Ria was struck by the difference in the man since she last saw him. Admittedly, in 1996 he'd been a few years off retirement, but he'd still looked young and vital. The man before her had a curve of the shoulders that suggested age and his hobbling gait attested to some issue with either hips or legs. His eyes were still bright though, and when he saw her, he smiled wide.

The reunion was nice, they chatted about lots of normal and general things. Work, holidays and in Phil's case, grandchildren. It was only as their cups were half-empty that Ria dared mention the link that bound them in friendship.

'He's never left me alone you know. I mentioned years ago the flowers and things, well it never stopped. Even when I moved house, moved job, he always left things. Even now I have a video doorbell, the things that have been dropped off have been dropped by someone who covers their face and doesn't seem to be traceable. I've pretty much given up on reporting it now, nothing ever happens. It's why I'm here actually. I feel like, if I can get some kind of closure, I'll be able to move on better. I just need to say a proper farewell to Marc and acknowledge all the things that happened here. I'm only here for a few days but hoping I can find some sort of peace.'

'I get that Ria. If you still think he's following you though, you should still tell the police. What if he tried to take you again?'

Ria shook her head at him, he was always worrying. 'If

he was going to take me again, he'd have done it by now. I'm not so much scared of him now, I don't think he wants to hurt me. I still want him gone though'.

Ria watched as Phil nodded his understanding but said nothing. They both quietly sipped at their drinks in a comfortable silence until eventually Ria decided it was time to go. 'It's been good to see you Phil. And thank you. Thank you for doing everything you could'.

Ria stood as she spoke, indicating her intention to leave. She watched Phil struggle to his feet and enclose her in a warm hug. 'I probably won't be down this way again Phil, but stay in touch alright?'

He nodded, releasing her from the embrace and smiling. 'Take care Ria and be careful not to go chasing ghosts, they won't help you'.

'I'm not chasing Phil, I'm here to say goodbye and move on'. As she spoke, she could feel a slight quiver in her voice and the prickle of tears starting in her eyes. She said goodbye again and left, waving through the window at Phil who had reclaimed his seat.

***

Ria stood on the soft sand, remembering the events of thirty years before. She lowered herself down, sitting and staring out to sea, tracing the mis-shaped fingers of her left hand through the sand. There was no pain in her hand anymore, but her fingers had never regained their normal shape. Being in this place, the memories flashed through her mind like movies. Unexpectedly vivid was the image of her friends, dancing around on the beach without her, wearing their tiaras and clutching their wands, laughter laced through every movement. It irritated her at the time, made her feel like an outsider, but now she looked with fondness at the silly innocence, the very last of it before the world changed forever. Thinking of her friends and the night she was taken, she could almost taste the limoncello they'd been swigging in the club before it all went wrong.

She had survived her ordeal, just. She'd tried so hard to live her life, but no matter how much she moved forward, she was always drawn back here. Back to the moment her life changed and the place where the first man she had loved had not been so lucky. He would never leave this place and though she hated to return, she couldn't leave him behind forever. She grieved the person she was before too. Not her exactly but her joyful naivete, and ability to just laugh and not feel the constant tension inside that would never leave her now.

Looking back up to the promenade, Ria could see the neat little houses, painted in pastel shades, were now dotted with flaking paint and decay from years of the harsh conditions so close to the sea. Some of the tiny shops were boarded up and had long since closed. The knowledge of trauma in the small town forever held in the memory of its buildings, in its very bones.

The bunting along the promenade was now tattered in many places, the colours faded beyond recognition. In that summer long ago, the people seemed young and vibrant, laughter and cheer emanating from every direction. Now the benches were full of old people, looking back, just like her. Sour faces prowled the streets of their town which had been tainted when it was in its prime and had never quite recovered.

Having drawn their initials in the sand, *RR + MD*, Ria laid back, sinking into the soft powdery beach and wondering how life could have been. The sensible side of her knew that her and Marc would have probably broken up before too long, probably by the end of university, but the other part of her loved to wonder. If they had stayed together, could they have made it work? Would they be married with children by now? Was the memory of Marc the thing that stopped her properly settling down with someone else? She'd told herself her relationships just weren't right, but maybe she'd just never moved on from here.

It had been nearly thirty years, but she still ended up back in those caves in her dreams. The feeling of elation when she emerged and was free, before the crashing pain of Marc's death had touched her. Maybe they could have escaped together, if she'd made other choices.

She had returned to this place several times over the years and watched and waited and regurgitated her memories of that time.

Sitting and looking out to sea, her eyes scanned left towards thc cliffs and the sea caves. Each time she'd come here, she had wondered about those caves. She'd wanted to go back. She couldn't quite quantify why but she felt she'd never heal unless she went back to the caves.

Her eyes were dry as she slowly peeled off her clothes until she was sitting in a vest and underwear. She left her clothes and bag piled on the sand and walked slowly along the shoreline, gently submerging as she went, until she dived forward and swam. The sea was calm, a gentle push and pull but easy to swim through. She swam out first and then around the shore where she stopped. Hair slicked and eyes drawn wide, she stared back at the rock face and low opening, right at the level of the water, only visible as the sea drew back each time. Swimming with her head low in the water, eyes laser focused, Ria approached the rock face in smooth strokes. When her hands reached out and touched the rock, a sharp edge dug into the flesh of her hand. She winced, then her lips pulled out into a grim smile. She smeared blood on her cheeks, ready to battle with old ghosts. She sucked air deep into her lungs and then was gone. She'd ducked into the tunnel and headed in, pulling herself forward with the grit and regret of thirty years. She didn't feel the chill of the water or the sting of salt in her eyes She only felt the need to propel herself forward. When she emerged in that cave, light streaming from high above she felt heat inside, warmth in her heart like she'd left it here and was finally reunited.

She'd never really cried at the time. Not after the first day she was found, and not since. Perhaps the odd, lonely tear, but not the barrage of emotion she really needed to release. Until now. Emerging into that space that had haunted her for so long, the tears sprang from her eyes like rivers, and she laughed through them, the relief of release, an explosion of emotion. She had hauled herself from the water and onto the rocky ledge, laying back and looking up. Up at the rocky heights and what now seemed an impossible climb. The inner walls rising around her were worn smooth. If she'd tried to climb, she would have fallen and probably never escaped either. She wondered whether it would have been better that way, if that was what was supposed to happen.

She screwed her face up, shaking her head from side to side 'NO!' she screamed, and listened as it echoed around her. Heaving herself up, she squatted on the edge of the water wondering why she'd ever felt the need to come back.

She slipped into the water, aiming to leave and finally felt like she could put this place behind her, another deep breath and down she went. As she swam through the narrow tunnel back to the real world, something snagged at her shoulder and dislodged a large rock, it fell and landed on her back, pinning her down, unable to move either forward or backwards. She panicked and flailed her arms and legs in a flurry of bubbles and terror until, as her breath was about to expire, she stilled. An arm stretched out in front of her, still reaching to find herself, whoever she now was.

As the life was drifting from her, she thought she saw a shape coming toward her. She thought for a moment it was Marc, and that she was dead already and he was waiting for her. When the face got closer, she realised who it really was. Of course it was him, she couldn't even die without his eyes on her.

46 – Phil Campbell – 10/06/2025

Phil Campbell sat in a new and minimalist coffee shop. He watched as Ria walked away, happy to have seen her again after all the time that had passed. Something was still missing though. She still had that edge of sadness that she'd never shaken after her experiences twenty-nine years ago. She was better at hiding it now, she'd become better at masking her expression, but it didn't fool him.

He watched as she rounded a corner heading towards the beach and drained the last dregs of his now cool coffee. He was trying to decide whether to order another or head home. His wife was away for the day seeing friends so there was nothing to rush home for. He'd had problems with his legs recently and even a short walk drained him. He decided to put off the return journey for another half an hour.

He ordered another drink, a chai latte, which felt very trendy compared to his usual beverages. Lowering himself back into his comfy chair by the window, he took a newspaper that had been abandoned on the table and began flicking through. Same old rubbish, he thought. He was so fed up of the sensationalised trash that seemed to pass for news these days. Laying the paper on his lap he stretched. His arms reached wide, and he sucked in great lungfuls of air until he almost choked. There, in the street outside, walking in the same direction that Ria had, was a man. He was older than Phil remembered but something about his walk caught his attention. He'd tried to explain his 'coppers nose' to people before, the instinct built from years of fighting crime. He just knew something was amiss. He thought the man was trying not to be noticed. Phil noticed him though and it took him a few moments to react, before he accepted what he was seeing. Yes, he was older, but the man was certainly Jasper Stone.

Phil jumped to his feet before moaning from the pain in

his knees. He started to hobble to the door and then reality hit. There was no way he'd catch up to Jasper and Ria now. He pulled out his phone and frantically called Ria. It went straight to voicemail and his heart sank. If he let her get taken again, he didn't think he'd be able to forgive himself.

His finger hovered over his phone for a second longer before he jabbed three times at the nine. If he was wrong then so be it, he wasn't though, he knew it. He tried to explain to the operator that he needed police attendance but as he wasn't exactly sure where Ria or Jasper had gone, the operator said she needed a location. In the end. Phil gave his own location at the coffee shop. He hoped he could then go with the officers that turned up and identify Jasper if seen.

The five-minute wait felt like hours and despite the pain in his knees, Phil couldn't sit still with the adrenaline pulsing through his veins. He kept dialling Ria but each time, it went straight to voicemail. When a young officer eventually arrived, he didn't seem to possess the urgency that Phil expected. He clenched his teeth to prevent him saying something that would make the officer think he was a crazy old man.

'Hello sir, what seems to be the matter?' The young officer smiled as he spoke and Phil remembered being a young copper like him, talking to the oldies with what he thought was kindness but in fact read as condescension.

'I used to be a DI here. One of my old cases, an abduction and manslaughter, I've just seen the suspect. The victim in the case, Ria Roe is also in town. I'm afraid he's going to try to take her again. Please, let me hop in with you and see if we can find him.'

The officer looked unsure but after a moment, nodded his head. 'If we find him though, you stay in the car. Agreed?'

Phil nodded his agreement and hobbled out onto the

street with the officer. The police car was parked outside a neighbouring property, and they were quickly inside with the car slowly pulling away.

'He headed down there, on Bridge Street. It was a while ago now but I'm sure we can find him.' Phil leant forward, his knees were decrepit, but his eyes were still sharp.

Bridge Street headed down towards the beach with other roads joining and leaving at various junctions. The reality was, even if it was Jasper, he could now be anywhere. 'I'll head down to the beach first and work back up from there.' The young officer, PC Wilson said. 'You haven't got a picture of this guy then?'

Phil side-eyed PC Wilson, reminding himself to be kind and leave the sarcasm out if it. 'There are photos in the files, but it would take you a while to find them. I don't carry copies with me.'

There were parking spaces next to the promenade and PC Wilson parked and jumped out, eyes scanning the beach for anything unusual. 'She shouldn't be swimming out by those rocks, people get battered on them all the time.' PC Wilson's eyes took on a faraway look and Phil realised perhaps, even though he was still young, he'd still most likely seen some awful things while doing his job.

Before Phil could respond to his words, he allowed his eyes to follow where PC Wilson was looking. A small shape bobbed in the water to the East, close to the rocks. As Phil watched, the shape disappeared under the water. Phil knew in his gut that the shape was a person, he was also sure it was Ria.

PC Wilson was on his radio calling for coastguard assistance, he too was concerned. Looking again, hoping for the shape to re-emerge, Phil noticed something else. Another shape was moving fast through the water, swimming hard in the direction of what he thought was Ria. 'Oh god' Phil exclaimed before explaining to PC

Wilson that he thought Ria had swum out the caves where she escaped years before and that maybe the other shape swiftly approaching the spot she disappeared was Jasper.

'Coastguards are on their way', PC Wilson confirmed as they moved onto the sand, looking all around for anything that would confirm if the two shapes in the water were Ria and Jasper.

Down not far above the water line, Phil dropped down onto his backside in an ungainly way as he looked at a pile of clothes and a bag beside him. It was the clothes Ria had been wearing half an hour ago in the coffee shop and laid on top, there was a single yellow rose.

49 – Jasper – 10/06/2025

Watching became easier over the years. Jasper had managed to get tracking on Ria's car and phone and even put a tiny tracker in her handbag. The technology hadn't taken over, but it had removed some of the difficulties of trying to follow unseen.

Jasper had been sitting in his car in St Afan for half an hour. He would look for Ria soon but at the moment his phone showed that she was in a café nearby. He hoped he could 'bump into her' somewhere more isolated later. Once she left the café, he would try to get eyes on, he was always happier when in direct sight of her, rather than relying on a phone screen.

The little green dot labelled 'Ria' finally began to move down the road that led to the sea. The following now was easy and when Ria's dot finally stopped on the beach, Jasper put his phone away and strolled on towards the beach where he hoped to 'go old school' and get sight of her.

When his feet were curled into the sand he saw her. Waist deep in the sea and then diving forward and swimming. Jasper watched as she swam out and across to the caves. The caves he too remembered from all those years before. He could still taste the salty water as it came close to choking him. The wild panic at losing Ria but also fearing for his own life. A lot had changed since then.

He scanned the beach until he saw the small pile of Ria's clothes, neatly stacked on the sand. His head pivoted often, checking on Ria's progress as he slipped a gift for her on her clothes, while then stripping off his outer layers quickly. He was afraid for her. Afraid that maybe his continued presence in her life, albeit covertly, had driven her to a watery grave.

Jasper raced into the water, swimming hard, his chest heaving. As he entered the water, Ria bobbed beneath the waves and didn't rise again. Jasper felt his breath hitch, hoping she had entered the caves and not drowned. As he swam, he kept his eyes trained on the spot that Ria had vanished. He doubted he'd have found the right spot himself, or even if that was the same sport he'd emerged. It was all a blur. The waves carried him up then down in a constant rhythm, but his eyes remained fixed on his target.

Treading water to settle his breathing, Jasper glanced behind him. The bright sunshine bounced off the cars parked behind the promenade, but one car caught his eye. A police car, with an officer or two, he wasn't sure, stood outside. One of them was shading his eyes and seemed to be looking in Jasper's direction, before heading down onto the sand. Breathing deep, Jasper dived down beneath the surface and felt the irresistible pull towards the rocks. Arms outstretched to protect him from a headlong collision, he drifted closer until Ria's face emerged before him. She was just closing her eyes, the life drifting away. Jasper reached out and even in her last moments, he thought there was a slight recoil. He could see that she was trapped, unable to move either back into the cave or out. She was dying and it wrenched at Jasper's insides. He couldn't leave her here alone. He snaked his arms in and around her, trying to free her. He felt the tightening in his chest as his lungs screamed for more oxygen, but he refused to leave without her. He wove his arms in the gaps he could find and curled into her body. Glad to finally be able to get this close again after all this time. Cheek to cheek, he felt his consciousness ebbing and hugged her closer. Satisfied to end their tale like a proper love story.

50 – DI Phil Campbell – 11/06/2025

Once the call had gone in and the coastguard was on scene, Phil Campbell knew there was little else he could do. He sat on a bench, resting his aching knees while a hive of humanity buzzed around him. His eyes remained trained on the spot where he knew the caves lurked, just under the water level and out of view. Phil's mood switched frequently between numb and absolutely seething.

He heard the odd comment from those passing by. *I think the guy went in to save her. What a hero. So sad if the sea has taken them both.*

An endless prattle that mostly described Jasper Stone as some sort of hero. He could almost hear the headlines already and it made him nauseous.

Phil had been sat on the bench for at least a couple of hours. It seemed the rescue mission was more complex than expected. Further down the beach, Phil noticed a man with a camera hitched on his shoulder and a reporter with a microphone, wearing a solemn look in front of the camera. Bloody journalists, they always appeared when least wanted.

Phil got to his feet, stiff and uncomfortable. He began a slow hobble down to where the reporters stood. *We have been observing the rescue mission so far and have seen two bodies removed from the water at the same time. They seemed to be linked with arms entwined. We await a technical analysis, but it could be that these two bodies perished in some kind of loving embrace. We're yet to know if it was a suicide pact or a failed rescue mission, but what seems clear, at present, is that the two deceased parties died in the arms of someone they loved.*

'No, no, no!' screamed Phil.

'And you are?' asked the young man in front of the camera.

‘I’m an ex-police Inspector and a friend of hers’. The words died on Phil’s lips as he clutched at his chest. The tightness refusing to yield as he tried to suck in air and calm himself.

Slowly he was helped to the floor by the journalist, the shooting pain in his left arm confirming what he already knew was happening. The buzz of the nearby crowd fell silent, as the darkness crept in.

51 – DI Phil Campbell – 29/06/2025

The recovery had been slow so far, but Phil knew nothing would stop him from attending Ria's funeral. There had been a smattering of journalists in the street outside. Phil had glared but walked away. His chest wouldn't cope with the rage they would fuel. They'd updated the stories since the day of Ria's death when they reported it as some king of Shakesperean tragedy. Now they had dug into the original abduction case and smeared it relentlessly in the papers each day. They still suggested there was some kind of relationship between them though and nothing Phil did could make them drop that point.

He sat at the back of the church, listening to Ria's parents talk about their daughter. He scanned the crowd, expecting her friends, Callie, Molly and Olivia to be there somewhere. They weren't. A sadness filled his heart as he realised how little Ria had been able to move on with anything in her life. Anything except work.

Jasper abducted her and we all thought she'd escaped, but she never did. She'd been living with him in her head all these years, and there was nothing we could do to stop it.

THE END

Thank you for reading.

If you enjoyed these stories, please leave a review as I'd love to hear from you.

Please follow me on socials to be informed of new releases.

JDC

About the Author

J D Currums has had a passion for writing and storytelling for many years.

With a background in policing and a stint as the landlady of an Oxfordshire village pub, she has come into contact with many interesting characters that have become seeds of inspiration for the characters she creates.

Also, a keen artist, she is currently working on several projects both literary and artistic and is living in Caithness, in the far North of Scotland.

Follow on Facebook for details of new and current releases.

Author page: J D Currums - Author
Visit the shop at: www.payhip.com/jdcurrums
Reviews welcome on Goodreads

Acknowledgments

It takes a village to raise a child and a whole collection of people to complete a novel.

Firstly, huge thanks for patience, belief, support and sanity boosting, go to my husband Ian and our fantastic boys. It's taken a lot of my time and energy over the last year and they've supported me every step of the way with tea, cake and endless discussions about which characters to kill off.

A good writing friend and fellow author Susan Andrew has been a consistent source of positivity to counter my negative internal voice and provide critique and advice in the most helpful of ways. We have bonded over dark humour and a concerning search history about murder and body disposal.

The Solus Or critique group has been a source of both wisdom and inspiration and I'm so grateful for their tireless input. I hear you Helen, POV, POV, POV!

Jan Trezise – patience personified! A lovely human who has allowed this book to be more closely tethered with the English language.

Printed in Dunstable, United Kingdom

ˌ784660R00129